D1279482

...cabaret

Also by Lily Prior

La Cucina

Nectar

Ardor

An Imprint of HarperCollins*Publishers*

A ROMAN RIDDLE

Lily Prior

HarperCollins books may be purchased for educational, business, or sales promotional use. For information, please write: Special Markets Department, HarperCollins Publishers Inc., 10 East 53rd Street, New York, NY 10022.

FIRST EDITION

Designed by Claire Naylon Vaccaro

Library of Congress Cataloging-in-Publication Data is available upon request.

ISBN 0-06-077257-3

05 06 07 08 09 BVG/RRD 10 9 8 7 6 5 4 3 2 1

For Christopher

Contents

Cast

MYSELF, FREDA LIPPI (NÉE CASTRO)

FIAMMA, my sister

PAOLO BALBINI, the Detective

ALBERTO LIPPI, the ventriloquist

SIGNORA DOROTEA POMPI, proprietor of the Onoranze Funebri Pompi

PESCO, Fiamma's chauffeur

PIERINO, my parrot

POLIBIO NASO, a fool, becomes Fiamma's husband

UNCLE BIRILLO, my mother's brother

AUNT NINFA, Birillo's wife

SIGNOR NABORE TONTINI, my downstairs neighbor

THE PALUMBO TWINS, exotic dancers at the Berenice cabaret club

LUI MASCARPONE, doorman and general factotum at the Berenice

GLORIA FANTORELLI, snake charmer at the Berenice

DARIO MORMILE, impresario of the Berenice

AMALTEA
GENOVEFFA } *some of Alberto's voices*

MALCO, Alberto's dummy

MAMMA, my beautiful mamma, who perishes in a car accident

MARIA ASSUNTA, the superintendent of our building in the Via Giulia

SIGNOR FRANGIOSA, one of our neighbors

PORZIO POMPI, Signora Dorotea's husband

RUPERTO, Fiamma's first love

NORBERTO, another of Fiamma's early boyfriends

SIGNOR SALTINI, padrone of the Magnolia cabaret club, where Mamma sang

MIMI FINI, the female impersonator at the Magnolia

IVO, the double bass player in Mamma's band

VITTORIO BRUSCHI, Mamma's agent

NORMA, Vittorio's secretary

VALENTINA, Vittorio's strapping mistress

SIGNOR RUSSO, newspaper vendor

SIGNORA FOGNANTE, tripe seller

PAPA GIOVANNI

SIGNORA SEMIFREDDO

SIGNORA MANTELLI

} *neighbors in our building in the Via Giulia*

REMO, son of Maria Assunta, my first love

RAFFAELLO, Aunt Ninfa's hairdresser

SIGNORA PUCILLO, Aunt Ninfa's mother

DRUSILLA MORELLI, the sadistic physiotherapist

DR. BONCODDO, my first psychiatrist

NICODEMO, Dr. Boncoddo's lover

DR. FARRANDA, Dr. Boncoddo's boss

SIGNOR FELICE, Signora Pucillo's paramour

TELMA MACCARRONE, Signora Pucillo's love rival

GREGORY THE GREAT, the first pope buried by Signora Dorotea's forebears

SAINT PETER, appears as himself

CALIPSO LONGO, receptionist at the funeral parlor

SIGNORA FORTUNA, my first corpse

SIGNOR CREMOSO, ice cream vendor and would-be lover of Fiamma

MISENO NUMITORE, another of Fiamma's contestants

CUNIBERTO MORETTI, a relief pallbearer and vendor of vanilla pods, one of my first dates

ERNESTO PORCINO, inventor of weeping eyeballs, and my first would-be lover

LORETTA, Signora Dorotea's sister

SIGNORA PORCINO, Ernesto's wife

THE PORCINI, Ernesto's children

SIGNOR SETTEBELLO, a corpse

CLODIA STROZZI, my roommate on the cruise liner, the *Santa Domenica*

THE GREAT FANGO, the magician on the cruise

MEL CARTOUCHE, the international artiste

RULA ARGENTI, the source of the dysentery outbreak

FANTASIA SPIGA
NERO PUPA
NICOLETTA BELLINI } *third-class passengers*

SIGNOR STUFO, a corpse

SIGNORA STROZZI, Clodia's mother

SIRO, Signora Dorotea's holiday romance

SIGNORA DRUSILLA LIPPI, Alberto's mother

NUNZIATA, Alberto's sister

TUSCO GOZZINI, the notorious gangster

CARLO MARTELLO, the butcher in the Campo dei Fiori

GIANGIACOMO CAMPOBASSO, the hairdresser

MANILIA PIETRAPERTOSA, the lemon vendor

FAUSTO PAZZI
BERNEDETTA SORBOLITO
CRISPINO MONGILLO
} *bystanders in the Campo*

BRINI, security guard at the Banca di Roma

NINO, a talking hamster

POLIBIO JUNIOR, Fiamma's son

MAX CALDERONE, an alias used by the Detective

MAFALDA FIRPOTTO, a corpse whose body sprouts violets and who is hailed as a saint

SISTER PRISCA, mother superior of the Santa Fosca convent

PADRE BONIFACIO, priest to the sisters of Santa Fosca

MISS OLGA MOLLICA, singer at the Berenice

SIGNORA AGNELLO, a corpse

THE BUCO TWINS, proprietors of an undertaker's in the Via Ombrone

VERONIQUE KAPOOR, my stage name

...cast...

FRANCO
SELMO D'ANGELO
LABBRA FINI
— *members of the jazz band at the Berenice*

BEATA FRESCA, cocktail waitress at the Berenice

VALERIA
NERISSA
— *victims of the fire, and my neighbors in the sanitarium*

NURSE SPADA, a nursing sister on the ward

LOLA, Labbra Fini's girlfriend

DR. PICCANTE, another psychiatrist

NELLO TONTINI, son of my downstairs neighbor

GLORIA, Pierino's mate

MIMOSA PERNICE, Uncle Birillo's mistress

PERDITA STELLATA, proprietress of the pre-owned clothes stall

SELMO MANFREDI, the fishmonger

Now

one

I struggled up the stone steps clutching a plucked chicken to my chest. Squashed under my arm was the carton containing the new wig and the squeakers; my basket was laden with raspberries, red peppers, *pancetta*, and broad beans; and as I fumbled for my key in the string bag containing the library books, it came to my attention that my front door was cordoned off by tape. What could be going on? Was there wet paint? Nobody told me there was to be maintenance. I hesitated, and a tall man appeared in my doorway.

"Signora Lippi?"

I nodded.

"Please come inside, and try to remain calm."

He pushed the tape aside to allow me in. There was

scarcely room for us both in the narrow passage. I could smell the garlic and the anchovies from his lunch on his breath. Tiny globules of sweat clung to his upper lip. In the dim light he was inhaling me, and his eyes were glued to my chicken. They were a little bloodshot, and filled with hunger. His suit was rumpled. It was clear he was a detective.

"What is it?" I asked faintly. "Is it Fiamma?" My sister was scornful of the dangers she faced, but I had long lived in dread of a moment like this one.

"It's your husband, signora," he breathed, allowing my heart to start beating again. Fiamma was safe.

"He has been taken," the Detective continued, "and your apartment has been ransacked."

"Taken?" I repeated, not understanding him.

"He has been seized. Disappeared. You know the way things are, signora; it is unlikely you will ever see him again."

Alberto seized! It hardly seemed likely. I had heard about such disappearances, of course, but why would anybody want Alberto? It had to be a mistake. If he had been taken, they would soon realize their error and release him. I had no doubt he would be back in time for his supper, and this being Saturday, he would be expecting chicken with scorched pepper sauce.

As my brain raced ahead to tonight's dinner, the Detective

seemed to expand and fill the passage completely. I became aware, as we faced each other, that his body was now touching mine and his breathing was slow and heavy. The appearance of a second man emerging from the parlor filled the corridor beyond capacity. I was struck by the way the second man's earlobes had continued growing down the sides of his neck until they reached almost to his shoulders.

"I've finished, sir," he said, and pointed with his head to the clear plastic bag he was carrying. "Just some items we're taking away as evidence, signora." I couldn't be sure, but I thought I could detect some items of my underwear in the bag. What could they want with those?

The man in charge grappled for some time with his hand in his pocket. It felt as though he was examining my thighs, but it was only because we were all pressed so closely together. His subordinate was in fear for his wallet, I could tell. After a delay, during which time seemed to warp and stretch, he finally fished out a card and handed it to me. Like his suit, it was crumpled and slightly damp. Although the writing was smudged, I could make out the words, "Paolo Balbini, *Polizia Municipale,* Roma 17," and a number at headquarters.

"It is unlikely they will try to contact you, signora," he said, "but if they do, or even if they do not, you have my number."

Finally they squeezed out past me onto the more spacious landing. The backward glances Signor Balbini threw me showed how much it hurt him to leave. I said nothing, but shut the door behind them.

My brain, and my mouth, seemed both to have dried up. It felt like a dream. Just a few minutes ago everything had been normal. It was Saturday. I had gone into work for a couple of hours—there had been a number of murders during the night, and Signora Dorotea needed my assistance in masking some bullet holes and reconstructing a nose that had been blown off in an explosion. Then I met Fiamma for coffee at Bobrini's. She had just returned from a fact-finding mission to Bolivia, and was covered in ulcers from poisoned fish served at the official banquet. She couldn't face any food, so I ate all the *pasticcini* myself and I have to say they were delicious. Then she was driven away by her chauffeur, Pesco, to an emergency summit at the Ministry, and I ran my errands. I returned my library books, and picked out three new ones, collected Alberto's order from the theatrical trickster's in the Corso, took my funeral suit into the dry cleaner's, and then did my shopping at the market stalls in the Campo dei Fiori.

Every Saturday was the same. Now this.

I walked through the rooms with the feeling I was acting a part in a film. Everything was in such a mess. It was as though a huge and hideous monster had swallowed my contents and regurgitated them, partially digested. It was awful, but worse was to come: when I stumbled into the parlor, I found Pierino's cage overturned and empty. Frantically I searched the ruins, but he was gone. I ran to the windows, squinting into the sunlight, to try and spot him, but there was no sign of him. Opposite, slouching in the doorway of the Belbo Forno, I identified the form of Detective Balbini. He was looking up at me, and hurriedly I slammed the shutters.

I had to find Pierino. I didn't know how long he had been missing, but there was a chance he could still be nearby. I flew down the stairs and out into the street. I didn't bother to lock the doors; any thief who could find something of value among the chaos was welcome to it.

I raced into the Campo, scattering the flocks of flea-bitten pigeons. The market had closed up by now, for today I had been later than usual, but its slimy traces remained: pigs' eyes and poultry claws, fish tails and innards, frothing puddles, guts and gore. The stench was terrible after the sun had been on it. I prayed Pierino had not landed near any of the butchers' stalls: some of them, I knew, would take a cleaver to anything. I looked about me for traces of azure feathers; thankfully there weren't any.

Over by the fruit stalls a fat man in orange overalls poked

with a hairless brush among the debris of deformed bananas and dead figs disguised as squashed dormice. Broken watermelons splayed their guts in the gutters, and bruised nectarines and punctured pomegranates swam among them. The stench of fermenting fruit was thick and heady, and I thought I stood a good chance of finding Pierino here.

"Have you seen a blue parrot?" I asked the road sweeper.

"I see nothing," he replied with a menacing movement of his stumpy brush.

I ran along scanning every window ledge and waterspout and fountain, every column, statue, lamppost, railing, parked car, and *motorino*. I called to Pierino softly, coaxingly. I scooped up palmfuls of the fruity goo to tempt him. I became covered in a sticky, stinking mess. I tensed my ears for the sound of his voice. Like this, straining my senses, I examined every street and alleyway in the district. Sometimes, I felt sure I was being watched, but whenever I looked round, I couldn't see a soul. In fact, the streets were strangely deserted, and that was a bad sign.

Hours passed and I hadn't caught so much as a glimpse of Pierino. I was exhausted and began to feel hopeless. He could be anywhere by now. Dejected, I headed back toward the apartment. It was getting late and in the half-light it was difficult to see anything. I would look again tomorrow, although

I prayed Pierino would, by then, have found his own way home.

I did wonder what would be waiting for me this time as I entered my building. My first choice would have been that it had all been a dream: I would find Pierino in his cage, the apartment neat and tidy, and, I suppose, Alberto demanding his *pollo*.

"Pierino?" I called hesitantly from the door. There was no answer. "Alberto?" Again nothing. I prowled through the rooms, terrified of what might be lying in wait for me. I knew what went on. Why, every day at work we dealt with the brutality of the city's gangsters: severed heads, limbs, private parts. Although I'm not squeamish, I shuddered at the thought. Alberto's parts were unattractive enough while still attached to his body. Then I noticed something strange. On the pillows of the bed there lay a red rose. It hadn't been there before, I was sure. I fingered its velvet petals and put it to my nose: its perfume was so intense it was overwhelming. This was weird: but it was better than finding a horse's head, or indeed, Alberto's.

Despite my exhaustion, I began to set things straight. It was better to be occupied than to sit brooding. The apartment seemed so empty without my precious Pierino. Sadly I put the half-pecked figs and plums back in the bottom of his cage for when he came home. I didn't allow myself to think he might not return. Tomorrow I would make posters and stick them up all over. I would offer a reward. That way the entire population of the city would be out looking for him.

I found the telephone hiding under a pile of puppets, and decided to call Fiamma with the news. The Secret Service operator answered, and I gave the various passwords to connect me to her home number. Finally she answered with the coded phrase:

"It's the eggplant that tempts me."

"Pierino's gone," I said.

"He'll come back," she said, although I could tell from the tone of her voice she didn't care.

Then I told her the shocking business about Alberto.

"That's the best news I've heard in ages," she said; then I heard her clamp the phone to her chest as she shouted to Polibio, "Great news, that *puzzone* Freda married has been dispatched." Then I heard Polibio cheering, corks popping, and glasses clinking.

"Forget that little creep, Freda," she continued; "don't give him another thought. Find someone else, and don't make the same mistake again."

"Yeah, forget him," drawled the voice of the Secret Service detail who was listening in.

"The guy was a dork," chipped in the operator.

I hung up. Then I called Signora Dorotea, and Uncle Birillo. He was still at his office even though it was late on Saturday night. Their reactions were the same as Fiamma's. It was as though they were all reading from the same script. They all assured me that Pierino would come back, and could not repress their joy that Alberto had gone.

After I replaced the receiver, immediately it rang again, making me jump. Suppose it was the abductors? Should I answer it? Or let it ring? I looked around the room, but there was no help to be had. The lemons restored to their fruit bowl kept their views to themselves. The mirror reflected an outward scene of calm that belied the whirl of thoughts passing through my head.

Shrilly, the phone rang on. Whoever it was was certainly persistent.

"Answer that phone," screamed Signor Tontini from his window beneath mine. "Answer that phone, I say." He seemed on the verge of an apoplectic fit. His doctors had warned him, but it was no use: rage was all that was keeping him alive.

Finally I picked up the receiver. Then I almost dropped it; I was so nervous. At first there was just the grainy sound of a bad line, typical in the city at that time. I held my breath. What would be their demands? Would I hear Alberto being tortured? Hear his screams as he was having his bits chopped off? My hand trembled as I held the phone to my ear. Then there came the sound of music. An old show tune Mamma used to sing. He was being tortured in time to music. It was grotesque.

"Tell me, tell me, tell me you love me."

I was on the verge of hanging up. I couldn't bear it. Then a voice came on the line. Between bursts of the music I could hear it saying:

"Yeah, put the Palumbo twins on again. . . . I don't care, they'll have to go on again. . . . Fuck the wig; if it's gone she'll have to go on without it. . . . Just get them on the stage, Lui, now . . ."

None of it made any sense, yet there was something about the desperate, incoherent voice I recognized. I was shocked, then, to hear the voice address me by name.

"Freda, you there?"

It didn't wait for me to reply, but continued immediately:

"Where the fuck is Alberto? He hasn't shown up tonight. The punters are getting restless. Gloria Fantorelli has been on three times. They're throwing the food. The regular chef was shot on his way in. We're doing our best here—no, they can't have their money back—I'm having to put the twins on again. Tell him to get his butt down here now, or it's the end of the line for him and the dummy, you hear me, Freda?"

Of course, it was Dario Mormile, the impresario of the Berenice cabaret club where Alberto performed on a Saturday night. He didn't even bother to listen to the whole of my explanation before there was a crunch and the line went dead.

I put the phone back on its cradle. It had been a false alarm. But my heart was still beating irregularly. I almost rang Detective Balbini but decided against it. He confused me, and besides I had nothing new to say. Instead, I put the raspberries into a bowl, went into the bathroom, and ran a hot, deep, bubbly bath. I peeled off my fruit-stained clothes and stepped into the tub, balancing the raspberries on my knees. I scooped up a handful and pressed them into my mouth with dripping fingers. They were sublime. The juice dripped down my chin and dropped into the water creating pink curlicues.

The hot water seeped into every space in my body, and soothed me. I hoped the steam would smooth out my crumpled thoughts like creases in linen, but it didn't: I remained totally bewildered. The only thing I knew for certain was that I didn't want Alberto back.

three

That night I slept better than I had in the three years since our marriage. I left off the impervious nightgown I wore to repel Alberto's halfhearted advances and lay naked in the center of the bed with all the pillows beneath me, stretching out my fingers and toes to the farthest corners, where the sheets were deliciously cold. Usually I was left with a narrow strip along the edge: all that was left unoccupied by Alberto.

I didn't miss the voices either—the voices of Alberto's act. They had always played a part in our relationship. Soon after our disastrous wedding night, through these voices, I was to learn of his affairs.

A soft female voice would come from the pillow right beside me.

"Alberto," she would croon. "Do that again. Once more, I implore you." Then she would laugh a low, sultry laugh.

Soon Alberto would call out in a mushy voice, one that was his own:

"Oh, Amaltea."

Or:

"Oh, Genoveffa."

What these women saw in him, I'll never know.

In the night, that big, empty night, although I was asleep, I was conscious of the heat intensifying. I kicked off the covers to expose my naked form to the cool air. The slightest feathers of the breath of air too frail to be called a breeze came through the open windows and caressed me. In the heat, the perfume of the mysterious rose throbbed and drenched the air with its scent. I bathed in it, and as I bathed, I dreamed.

In the confused perspective of the dream, Detective Balbini had come into the bedroom. It didn't seem strange to me that he should be there. Indeed, it was almost as though I was expecting him. His scent vied with that of the uncanny rose, and made me lurch in the pit of my stomach. I had always been particularly sensitive to odors; why then, I had often asked myself, had I married Alberto, who carried about him the whiff of something unpleasant, something incompletely masked by an astringent brand of disinfectant he kept locked in the bathroom cabinet? The Detective smelled of passion, of yeast, sun-ripened skin, an animal scent that spoke to the empty space inside my body. I was drowning in it.

In the darkness, which was incomplete on account of the fullness of the moon outside, I saw his hungry eyes feed upon me. His Adam's apple rode up and down his neck like the slider on a trombone as he swallowed hard several times. I saw him pass a hand slowly over his face stretching his features into a rubber mask. Then he ripped off his jacket like a life-saver and dived alongside me into the bed. There was a jolt as one of the legs of the divan punctured the floorboard beneath, but now was not the time to worry about it. To stifle the complaints from Signor Tontini, whose own bed lay immediately beneath, I threw myself on top of the Detective and kissed him roughly on the mouth. His hands reached around the back of my head and pulled me into him. His tongue filled my mouth. I couldn't breathe. I felt surges lurching through my body, bubbling up from deep down inside, shooting along my arms and legs. It was like that time I got an electric shock in the Laundromat. But better.

I couldn't believe what was happening to my body, and I never wanted it to end. I sandwiched the Detective's face between my hands and kissed on as though my life depended upon it.

Burning kisses I had read about in my library books. These were they.

I became aware of the Detective's hands straying over my body. The pads of his fingers, the lightest trace of a fingermail, wrote their sensuous script upon me. They wrote of tantalizing secrets, endless journeys, imagined places. His touch was alternately stroking, soft as a whisper, then probing and pressing, urgent and vibrato, sliding home. I abandoned myself to him, escaping from myself, from the past, from everything real, and from the cursing of Signor Tontini, which was rising up in bubbles of invective and which my ardor was working valiantly to ignore.

I clawed at his shirt. Polyester. So durable. The bitter enemy of lovers. But I wouldn't let it defeat me. Summoning the strength stored by my years of starved passions, I tore it away by the collar and almost garroted him with his tie. The sleeves clung feebly to his arms, but his torso was bare. His chest was a Persian carpet of dark hairs, and I sank my breasts into its pile, making him moan and mew.

I had to remove his pants. The situation had become desperate. Their very existence now caused me a physical pain. Both he and I struggled to loosen them. The belt was done up way too tight. We scrabbled and strained, wrenched and wrestled. Finally, just as we were losing hope, the belt buckle capitulated and I was able to tear down the pants, but of course, the Detective, in his haste, had left his shoes on, and they were now hopelessly stuck in his inside-out pants. I leapt from the mattress onto the floor. Through the chink of light coming through the broken board, I could discern the enraged and elasticized face of Signor Tontini, peering upward. Thankfully the darkness above prevented him from seeing me.

I turned my attention once more to the pants. I was conscious that unless they came off soon, the evening would be ruined. They had assumed too prominent a role already. Now that my blood was up, I thought I would have the strength to rip my way past the shoes. I dug my feet into the floor for added leverage. The Detective gripped the bedpost. And I began to pull. I pulled and pulled. The Detective gritted his teeth. Then with one final yank, which took more strength than I knew I had, they came free, but I ricocheted across the room, was flung against the closet, cracked my head against it, and woke up.

I was dazed, but not badly hurt. What a ridiculous fantasy! I wanted to laugh. The Detective, of all people! I had always been prone to bizarre dreams, but this one won a prize.

Yet when I heard a voice emerging from the darkness, I felt a jolt like another electric shock. Was it Alberto and his menagerie of voices come back?

"Quickly, my angel, my darling," said the voice, thick with desire, "hurry and get back into the bed."

Even in the beginning, on the cruise liner, Alberto had never spoken to me in a voice that made me wrinkle uncomfortably inside. What could be going on? Despite the blow to my head, I got up and lunged at the light switch. As the glare flooded the room and bit at my eyes, I honestly could not believe what I saw. Yes, it was Detective Balbini, in the flesh, actually in my bed, gaping and blinking in the cruel blaze of light, and wearing nothing but his shoes and knee-length nylon socks.

Was I going mad? Or was I still asleep and still dreaming?

"My sweetheart, why do you turn on the light? Is it not a little bright, this way? Still, whatever pleases you. Come here, I implore you, come back to the bed."

I watched, appalled, as he got up and started to come toward me, his arms wide. His thing was purple, and pointing straight at me. It reminded me of the one belonging to Ernesto Porcino that I had fondled clumsily back in the summer of 1971.

"You," I stuttered, shielding myself with the tattered scraps of the pants still in my hand. "What are you doing here?" What could he be doing there?

Before he could answer, there came the sound of splintering wood. The blade of an ax came up through the floor, chopping the space between us, severing the moment, and stopping the Detective dead in his tracks.

"Whore!" spluttered the rage-filled tones of Signor Tontini. "Her husband is disappeared, and the same night, the very same night, she gets in a replacement. Can you believe it? I ask you. What a whore. What a strumpet . . ."

There followed more blows of the ax and a chasm opened up in the floor, revealing more of Signor Tontini glowering beneath.

I witnessed the Detective's ardor dwindling. Casting me a glance that contained the slow smoldering heat of his desire, his desperation, his frustration, and his suppressed fury at the interruption, he shielded with his cupped hands the once purple thing that had dulled to a limp pink, and ventured toward the hole that had opened up between our feet.

"Signor," he addressed Signor Tontini, in a strangulated voice that contained every drop of his pain, "Paulo Balbini of the Roma police department. I have no alternative but to arrest you for possession of an offensive weapon with intent to cause injury. I warn you not to resist arrest. I will be with you shortly."

The spasm of rage that subsequently erupted from Signor Tontini was enough to convince me that his spleen could not hold out much longer. I knew he would be dead on arrival at the police station.

I was equally convinced the Detective couldn't wear his own pants. They were in ribbons. Once I had secured my robe around my flesh, which was roasting with embarrassment, I rummaged in the closet and produced one of Alberto's garish costumes. It was a violent blue sateen with red velvet trim and had been made to measure by the tailor Rinaldi near the Piazza Borghese.

The Detective climbed into the pants willingly enough, but it quickly became apparent that he and Alberto were wildly dissimilar in stature. Still, they had to do: he was not in a position to be particular. Teamed with his own jacket, which was still relatively undamaged, he looked completely ridiculous.

He stepped carefully across the minefield my floor had become, holding the pants up around his middle like a clown. At the front door he turned and kissed me shamelessly.

"I will be back as soon as I can, my darling," he murmured passionately, his stubble grazing my cheek, the smell of his hormones deep and indecent. "Wait for me. I will not disappoint you."

Moments later, through the hole in the floor, I saw Signor Tontini being led away in handcuffs as meekly as a lamb. Perhaps he was pleased someone was finally taking him seriously. After they had gone, I shunted the bed over the hole. Unfortunately the ax had chopped off the leg that had gone through the floor, but a pile of books restored the balance.

The valise containing Malco, the dummy, had been dented in the skirmish, and I could hear him muttering, "Whore. Strumpet. Whore. Strumpet." I gave him a kick to silence him, and in doing so bruised my bare foot. Soon, I knew, I would send him to the junk shop in the Largo Febo. But before that time could come, he would already have disappeared.

I gathered up the scraps of Detective Balbini's clothing. They were suffused with his erotic odor. I didn't know what to do with them, so I shut them up in the bathroom. I drank a long glass of cool water and then lay down, but of course I couldn't rest. I was a balloon about to burst. Inside I felt a throbbing, a dampness, and that familiar itchiness that had no respite. It was my destiny to suffer always from acute sexual frustration. If only I had married a real man, like the Detective, I believe my life would have been different. But I had married Alberto, and had only myself to blame.

Then

one

It wasn't difficult to identify exactly when everything had gone wrong. It was June 5, 1965, the worst day of my life, past and future.

I still recall every minuscule detail. It was my sixteenth birthday, and overnight a rash of scarlet spots had picked its way over my face. These pimples persisted until September 17, 1970, a Thursday, by which time I had grown so used to them that I scarcely recognized myself without them.

As a special treat, for breakfast, we had little cakes from the *Pasticceria Sottosanti,* and I opened my presents. Mamma had long since promised that for Christmas I would be given the parrot I had craved since I was seven and, in preparation, for my birthday gave me a book entitled *The Care of Tropical Birds*. She also gave me a yellow bathing costume, a tiny brooch in the shape of a butterfly, a journal in which to record the interesting details of my life, and a bottle of pink nail polish. Fiamma, presciently, but tactlessly, gave me a tube of boil ointment, which I slathered on, but it didn't work. From Aunt Ninfa and Uncle Birillo there was a hideous crocheted cardigan with matching socks, and from Maria Assunta downstairs, a box of violet-flavored candies.

We were going to spend the day at the beach, and I started preparing the picnic. There were all my favorite things: hot bread, a roast chicken, a whole mozzarella cheese, a honeycomb, wild strawberries, a bottle of cherryade (the sort that tastes like medicine), and a massive bar of chocolate, which I nibbled while I worked (in fact, I had already eaten half of it, but it was my birthday, after all).

I had just finished packing the basket when there came from the street the relentless honking of a horn, like the blast from a ship. It was Fiamma driving Uncle Birillo's new car. It was American, an Oldsmobile Cutlass convertible, huge and red. He had won it in a contest, and his smiling picture had appeared in the newspapers. In a reckless moment he had agreed to let Fiamma borrow it when she passed her driving test, and now that she had, he could only watch fearfully as she surged down the slope of his garage, and hurtled along the street.

Now Mamma was finally ready. She was so glamorous. Something I sadly didn't inherit. In fact, I believe I was born a frumpy dresser. Yes, I never saw Mamma without her false eyelashes on, and her face and fingernails perfectly painted, even when she was washing the dishes, except, of course, for that last time in the hospital, when she lay dying: broken and disfigured. This morning she was wearing a green dress with white polka dots, and a black pillbox hat with a veil that just covered her eyes. Long gloves, high-heeled shoes, and a trailing cloud of Donna Misteriosa completed the outfit.

We clattered down the stairs to find a crowd gathered around the car. Small boys sucking lollipops were smearing the paintwork with their sticky fingers. A peddler was trying to interest Fiamma in the contents of his tray: jumping beans, false noses, hair restorer, colored chalks, and sticks of licorice. Passersby were leaning in, probing the red leather upholstery and twiddling the dials on the dashboard.

When Mamma appeared, two young men rushed forward to get her autograph, for she was quite a celebrity in our neighborhood. Signor Frangiosa, who lived opposite, and who had had a crush on her for years, asked if he could take her photograph. Mamma posed on the hood for several shots, one of which was later to appear on the front of *Il Messaggero* along with a report containing all the gruesome details. Whoever could have predicted that the picture capturing Mamma on that gay and glorious morning was destined for such use?

So, we packed the picnic basket in the trunk, which was almost as big as our apartment; then I climbed into the back-seat, and Mamma got in beside Fiamma, who thrust her foot down hard on the gas pedal. The mighty engine let out a roar like a rocket, and the Cutlass leapt forward, scattering the schoolboys, and enveloping the crowd in a choking cloud of blue smoke.

"Fiamma, are you sure you can manage to drive something so large?" Mamma asked as she was thrown back in her seat.

"Of course," Fiamma answered scornfully, but it took a while for her to get the hang of it, and the vast vehicle bit and bucked as she danced on the foot pedals and poked at the controls, which were new to her.

Yet soon enough we had left the city behind and were coasting along smoothly with the sun beaming on our faces and the breeze ruffling our hair. Mamma started to sing "*Io So Perchè*," and I joined in. She had such a beautiful voice. She was still singing when the accident happened, when her song turned into the scream that I still hear sometimes in the dead of the night.

The white road shimmered in the heat. Fiamma drove

faster and faster. Houses, trees, oncoming traffic, pedestrians, dogs, and chickens, began to flash past and blur together. The dust rose up behind us. The wind whipped wildly by. Mamma held on to her hat.

At the bottom of the hill, still some way ahead of us, the figure of a little old man ran out onto the highway. When he became aware of the mighty Cutlass bearing down on him at an impossible speed, he froze to the spot, and began to scream.

The bubble Fiamma had blown into a big balloon burst, covering her face with exploded gum and obscuring her eyes. Her foot jabbed blindly for the foot brake but couldn't find it. Mamma was screaming. I was screaming. Fiamma was screaming. Seconds from certain death, the old man was screaming. By the roadside his middle-aged daughter, entrusted with his care, and whose back had been turned for no more than a second, was screaming too.

Time seemed to have stopped. There was just speed, and screaming. Nothing else.

At last, finally, but too late, Fiamma reached the brake. It was a heroic act. She put every last drop of her force and strength into stamping on it. Her whole body followed her foot into the well where the pedals were. She managed to bring the great hulking hungry beast to a halt a whisper short of the old man.

And, at the precise moment that the car stopped, Mamma took flight. I watched her soar up high into the air. Her shoes fell from her feet and flew away. Her hat, snatched up by a current of air, was carried out to sea and never seen again. The skirt of the green dress flared like a parachute, but it couldn't save her. Her hair escaped from its pins and streamed out behind her. I heard the tiny tinny sound of the pins falling onto the road. And Mamma was still screaming. Screaming. Screaming. Screaming. All the time I was watching in slow motion. I had been damaged, I felt vaguely, but I had been wearing the seat belt.

Mamma reached the height of her arc, and inevitably began to descend toward the earth. There was a slightly different note now in her scream. The force of gravity, perhaps, pulling it down a semitone. Her eyes were open wide, staring. They must have seen the ground rushing up to meet her. Trailing the washing she had ripped from a clothesline in passing, she was eventually brought to a halt by an enormous palm tree, into which she crashed, and into the rough hairy trunk of which her fine white front teeth sank.

The old man stopped screaming then. He had survived. But he lay down in the road in front of the car and died anyway, needlessly. His daughter collapsed and began frothing at the mouth. The car engine also gave up and died. Then there was a small but perfectly formed explosion, and licks of flame began to curl up and melt the paintwork.

Fiamma climbed out. She was unscathed, apart from a bloody mark on her forehead above the bridge of her nose. It was then that I closed my eyes and everything went dark.

two

Strangely Mamma didn't die instantly, although it would probably have been better for all of us if she had died there and then, in that fragrant garden, rather than in the hospital, where there was no beauty, no fragrance, no flowers, and no sunlight. Only sterile shades of gray, antiseptic smells, half-light, and silence. For a few hours, but no longer, she lingered on only to speak to us, to warn us perhaps, before she left us, entrusted to the care of her brother, Birillo, and his enormous wife, Ninfa.

I woke up when I felt someone slapping my cheeks. It was Fiamma. She was wearing the same pink T-shirt and shorts that she had been wearing when the accident happened, an eternity ago. She looked incongruous on the ward, like a day on a beach had somehow crept in among the serious business of death and disease and suffering. The mark on her forehead burned like a brand, and as she loomed in at me, I noticed she still had traces of the gum clogging her eyebrows.

"Freda, Mamma's calling for you. Come on." She uncovered me and looked at my battered body, appraising how she was going to move me. I couldn't feel anything, but my right leg had been broken and was in plaster from the thigh down to the ankle. My neck had suffered trauma from the whiplash and was encased in a brace. My head, which had been beaten repeatedly between the seats, was wrapped in bandages. My skull had been flattened slightly, but thankfully my brain was undamaged, although I was to suffer double vision periodically throughout my life.

"Come on, get up," said Fiamma without much patience, without any, in fact, and she proceeded to haul me into the wheelchair she had stolen from the adjoining ward of geriatrics. She ignored my howls of pain and bumped me up and down steps and along corridors until we arrived at the room where Mamma was waiting.

As we hurtled through the door (Fiamma pushed wheelchairs much as she drove, fearlessly and fast), we surprised an elderly priest who had been administering the last rites. He blessed us all with signs of the cross, and then, having given himself a thorough scratching, he limped away.

I couldn't believe the figure in the bed was my mamma. She was swathed in bandages like the Invisible Man. There were just slits for her mouth, nostrils, and eyes. Through the slits, she looked at me with love mixed with pain, sadness, pity, and resignation.

"My girls," she whispered; her voice was as broken as her body.

"You must be brave, and look after one another." She extended a hand to each of us, and they too were completely wrapped in bandages.

"Soon I must leave you, but I have so much to say to you first." Here she paused with the effort of speaking, and I was terrified she had already gone, because she was so quiet then, and I couldn't tell if she was breathing, and her cloth hands were weightless and limp and I didn't know what to do except cry.

But then she continued, quietly, and quickly, as though she was running out of time.

"Fiamma, don't feel bad about what happened. It wasn't your fault. It was the card that was dealt to you. You are destined for great things in your career, but you will marry a fool. Be happy. My Fredina, my sensitive one, I worry most for you. You too will be successful in your work, but you will have bad luck. Far in the future I see a ventriloquist, but no good will come of . . ." Here she broke off, but quite clearly hadn't finished the sentence. It was left hanging precariously in the air, and we waited in silence for her to continue. I don't know which of us realized first she had already gone.

Inside I was drowning, but outside I was quiet and still. There was an opening and shutting of a door behind me. A draft of air. I believe some people came in, and went away again. I gripped Mamma's hand and willed her not to leave me. I was too young to be an orphan. I felt if she tried hard enough, she could come back from the brink of death. But she didn't try.

Much later Fiamma said:

"I suppose I better take you back now."

"Not yet," I said. "I want to see her face."

"No you don't."

"Yes, I do, help me."

She hauled me to my feet and then went to smoke a cigarette in the corridor. She hadn't smoked before. Already she was developing bad habits.

"I want to remember her as she was," was what she said. But I wanted to know.

Carefully I began to unwrap the bandages, starting at the top of Mamma's head, peeling them away like the layers of an onion. I did see Mamma's face, but it wasn't the face I knew.

They tried to stop me from going to the funeral—the nurses, the doctors, Uncle Birillo—all saying that I wasn't strong enough, but I showed them. I even escaped from the hospital in order to visit Mamma in the Pompi funeral home. I made Fiamma push me there. She wouldn't come inside, so Signora Dorotea Pompi, who owned the business with her husband, Porzio, took control of the wheelchair and propelled me into the chapel of rest.

The transformation of Mamma was nothing short of a miracle. Signora Pompi was an artiste; there was no doubt of that. Mamma was restored to her beautiful self. I could hardly believe it. Her face was whole again, and so natural, not like a mask. Her eyes were closed, just as if she were sleeping, and her false eyelashes had been skillfully applied. Her lips were unblemished, plump, and rosy hued, and the husks of hair from the palm trunk that previously covered her face in a coarse and hoary beard had been painstakingly removed. Her hair, which had been mostly lost as she flew through the air, had been replaced and coiffed into an artful arrangement of sleek, cascading curls that tumbled across the pillow and trailed playfully over her shoulders.

I felt an enormous sense of relief, knowing that Mamma could now go to her grave with her head held high, and I was terribly grateful to Signora Pompi for giving her back her dignity. Later, in the reception area, the signora gave me a glass of lemonade and some honey cookies, and this was the first food I had eaten since the accident.

Later still, when I emerged, I discovered Fiamma on the opposite street corner with a gang of boys on *motorini* who looked dumb and dangerous. On the evening of the accident she had dumped her reliable steady, Ruperto, a medical student.

"There's no future for us," she had told him, before jumping on the back of a scooter with Norberto no-brain, who was widely known, even by his family, to be the most stupid youth in our district.

A few days later followed the funeral service, which took place at the Chiesa di Santa Griselda della Pancia, the little church dedicated to artists and entertainers. Finally heeding my pleas and my threats, Uncle Birillo had come to the hospital for me, bringing with him the mourning Aunt Ninfa had acquired: a dress with a wide sash and puffed sleeves, and a beret with an enormous pompom on the top. Every birthday and Christmas she got me little-girl's clothes, for she just couldn't accept that now I was sixteen, not six.

And so, arrayed like a teenage toddler, I was loaded into the back of a minivan for the journey across town. I was amazed to see that the sun was shining, that there were people walking about, that shops were open, conducting business as usual. Vendors advertised their wares in strident voices: "Rice fritters," "Artichokes," "Onions," "Chicken livers—fresh, fresh, fresh." A line of infants in pinafores crossed the street ahead of us, solemnly holding hands in pairs. Bicycles passed and pony carts jangling bells; cars and trucks zoomed by. A squashed rat lay in the gutter. There was the sulfurous smell of tar bubbling in a cauldron, the smell of drains, rotting garbage. The familiar pigeons were cooing and scratching. Everything was normal. Except my mamma was dead.

The street outside the *chiesa* was swarming with people, who parted to allow us through. Flashbulbs exploded in my face. Images of me were to appear in the evening papers, and I still have the cuttings, pasted into my scrapbook, alongside the obituaries. My mouth was open and my eyes were shut, and my damaged neck was bowed down by the weight of the giant beret on my head. I looked like a simpleton.

We seemed to be the last to arrive for the service, and the entire congregation turned to look as we came through the doors, the plaster cast first, me second, and Uncle Birillo third. Incense filled my nose, causing it to stream with mucus. I remember there were enough people inside to fill a football stadium. In fact, there weren't enough seats for them all, and many were forced to stand along the side aisles and at the back. We progressed at a suitably sedate pace in time to the requiem being sung by the choir, and it seemed to take forever. Lots of the ladies looked at me and burst into tears, causing their mascara to stream muddy streaks down their cheeks.

I recognized Signor Saltini, the *padrone* of the Magnolia club, where Mamma was the star. His eyes were raw from crying, and his impressive wart throbbed. He blew me a kiss, and then collapsed onto the false bosoms of Mimi Fini, the female impersonator with whom Mamma had shared a dressing room. There followed the whistling sound of air escaping though a puncture.

The members of Mamma's band, L'Elastico, stood shoulder to shoulder, sobbing in perfect harmony, their cries ranging from that of big Ivo, the double bass player, whose grief was resonant and deep, to the blaring wailing of Gianandrea, who was famous on the trumpet.

The chorus line had collapsed in a flurry of sequins and feathers and despair, the cocktail waitresses were in hysterics, and the barmen were bawling. There were so many regular patrons of the Magnolia in attendance that the small ones were obliged to sit on the laps of the bigger ones, and they comforted each other as best they could.

There were several celebrities present. I recognized immediately the man who played the alien in the movie *Galassia 17,* even though he didn't have the extra eye attached to his forehead, or the pointy ear extensions. Then I saw the man who read the news, the woman who predicted the weather, and the identical twins who appeared in the commercials for Zecca toothpaste. Mamma would have been really proud that all these famous people had come.

Further forward was Mamma's agent, Vittorio Bruschi, seated among his entourage: his secretary, Norma, who, from time to time, blotted his head with a powder puff; his strapping mistress, Valentina, whom he always passed off as his niece; and his tailor, his hairdresser, his masseur, his chauffeur, and his three-man bodyguard.

The rest of the pews were occupied by the people from

our neighborhood. There was Signor Russo, who owned the newspaper kiosk; Signora Fognante, who sold tripe from a tray balanced on her head; the toothless street sweeper whose name I never knew; and the crazy man who masqueraded as a monk and sang songs while washing his feet in our fountain. All the occupants of our building were there: Papa Giovanni, Signora Semifreddo and Signora Mantelli, and Maria Assunta and her son, Remo, whom I loved, furtively and hopelessly. When I saw them all—all dressed in their smartest clothes, all looking back at me with their eyes so sad—that's when I cried for the first time that day, and once I started I didn't stop.

At the far end, on a dais in front of the high altar, was the coffin of shiny wood, surrounded by arrangements of white flowers: lilies, roses, and dahlias. I felt sick seeing it there, knowing Mamma was shut up inside it.

Sitting with Aunt Ninfa in the front row was Fiamma. Although she had been pretending to be tough ever since the tragedy, sitting there she looked dwarfed and haunted, like a little frightened girl. Uncle Birillo parked me in the aisle, and I reached out to her. She fell into my arms and instantaneously we were wracked by sobs. Our aunt Ninfa joined in. She is truly the loudest woman I have ever known, and her trumpets of grief throughout the service were sometimes sufficient to drown out the words of the priest, and at times even the choir of matrons hired by Uncle Birillo at great expense.

Uncle Birillo's disapproving looks at his wife were not sufficient to silence her, in fact, their effect was quite the reverse. With a defiant gleam in her wet eyes she sobbed all the louder.

Trapped inside my brace and my plaster cast, I felt captive in a nightmare from which there was no waking.

As the matrons sang the Ave Maria, we filed in a line past the coffin. When her turn came, Aunt Ninfa kissed it and left a slimy slick of pink lipstick behind, like a snail's trail, which Uncle Birillo was only able to remove imperfectly with his pocket handkerchief.

Later, as they lowered Mamma into her grave, my heart felt as thin and lifeless as the long-dead lizard on the footpath that everybody had trodden on.

four

Later still when I was discharged from the hospital, I discovered I wasn't going home. Fiamma and I were to live with Uncle Birillo and Aunt Ninfa, at their apartment in Aurelio, in one of those soulless modern blocks overlooking the very same highway on which the accident happened, some twenty kilometers beyond, toward the coast.

Under protest, Fiamma was already there. Across the river, our own apartment in the Via Giulia had been stripped bare, and given up. It was now rented to a dentist with a wooden leg and a tenuous connection with Aunt Ninfa's hairdresser. There could be no going back.

Everything had changed so fast: it was as though our other life never even existed. I didn't even get the chance to say good-bye to anybody: to Signora Mantelli, who smelled of the aniseed balls she sucked and who knitted us mittens every winter; to Papa Giovanni upstairs, who cut for us figures out of folded paper with a pair of tiny scissors; and to Signora Semifreddo, who lived across the hall and who sobbed for ten minutes every afternoon at five. And downstairs, the building superintendent, Maria Assunta, who polished the floors of the communal areas until they reflected scenes so lustrous they seemed to contain in their glossy depths a life more vivid than that being lived above the surface. And, of course, Remo, lolling gracefully at corners, who appeared in my fevered adolescent dreams. I never saw him again.

At Uncle Birillo's, Fiamma and I were obliged to share the same small room for the first time in our lives. Thankfully, my uncle and aunt had no children (they hadn't been blessed, as Aunt Ninfa delicately put it), but they did have Signora Pucillo, Aunt Ninfa's mother, who had been a constant feature of their married life, even accompanying them as newlyweds on their honeymoon to Taormina.

Signora Pucillo did not relish the prospect of sharing the already cramped apartment with two teenage girls, one of whom she regarded as a murderer. She was the type of elderly person who views youth as a disease and is afraid of catching it. Still, with or without Signora Pucillo's blessing, we were installed in my uncle's apartment in the Via Gregorio Sette, and although it was scant consolation to her, we didn't like the arrangement any more than she did.

In those first few months after the accident Fiamma couldn't commit to anything. She gave up the place at teacher training college she had worked so hard to get, and for short bursts of time she applied herself to various occupations. For a few days she became a tourist guide at the Coliseum, but found the centurion's costume hot and heavy, and the helmet kept getting stuck on her head. Then she tried out as a kennel maid in a puppy farm, a blender in a glue factory, an artist's model, and a packer at a wholesaler of religious paraphernalia, a croupier in a nightclub, a biscuit taster, a window cleaner, and a rat catcher. The final straw came when she enlisted in the navy and packed her bags in secret.

That night, alone at last, and free from her nocturnal chuntering, I enjoyed the best night's sleep I had had since the accident. But for one night only. At dawn, with the gangplank partially drawn up, Aunt Ninfa besieged the port and stormed the ship, demanding the return of her niece. So Fiamma was dragged back to the suburbs, although her protests were in truth halfhearted. One night in the fetid dorm with eleven burly sailor girls had been enough to convince her she had made a huge mistake, and although she cried crocodile tears for Aunt Ninfa's benefit, in reality she felt like kissing her.

But my uncle and aunt had had enough of Fiamma's antics. The same day that she had been rescued from the *Nettuno,* Uncle Birillo exploited his connections at the Ministero degli Affari Esteri, and, in return for various favors, got Fiamma employed in a clerical position with good prospects and salary. Fortunately Fiamma took to the job, and over the years was able to work her way up to become a high-ranking civil servant with her own office, secretary, and, enviably, her own executive washroom. Once her talents became known to the bigwigs there was no stopping her, and she became involved in secret affairs, whose true nature was known only to Fiamma, a handful of people in Security, and the prime minister himself.

But here I am racing ahead of myself; back then, in the fall of 1965, although I did not share Fiamma's uncertainty about my occupation, I was in no state to embark upon it. Even after the bandages were removed from my head, the brace was taken from my neck, and the plaster cast was cut off my leg, I had to return to the hospital every weekday for treatment.

Yes, on Monday, Wednesday, and Friday mornings I propelled myself on crutches to the physiotherapy department. There, the sadistic therapist, Drusilla Morelli, manipulated my whiplashed neck with her brawny forearms until it cracked in submission, and I could feel a fug of fluid seeping around the base of my dented skull, which left me woozy and weak. Then, when my neck relented and accepted Drusilla Morelli's mastery over it, my poor mangled leg was subjected to torture by ice and a regimen of contortions for which it clearly wasn't designed.

My mental scars, of course, were less easy to heal. At night, I lay awake for hours listening to the cacophony of sounds issuing from Fiamma's sleeping form. She made more noise when she was asleep than when she was awake. And she was able to constantly surprise me with her variety. The grunts like an amorous gibbon; snores like the earth's crust rupturing; muted wails, groans, fervent whispers, chipmunk chomping; snorts, whines, whinnies. How much of this was due to the accident, I couldn't say, because nobody ever shared a bedroom with her before, but I am inclined to think that this was her natural state when sleeping, and that the tragedy had little or nothing to do with it.

My insomnia wasn't helped either by the restlessness of the city after dark, the ceaseless traffic on the Via Gregorio, the cacophony of sirens, the serenades of drunken lotharios, the howling of mad dogs, gunshots, fireworks, horns blowing, screaming, shouting, and general mayhem. I had never known such noise in our own apartment, in our sweet and gentle district across the river, but then again, I had never known insomnia either.

When I did manage to sleep, I was beset by terrifying dreams. Most often, we were back in the car, careering down the hill toward the old man who'd hurried into our path, and stood there gaping. I clearly heard Mamma's beautiful song transform itself on her lips into a scream with which the old man and I joined in horrible competition. Before the car could stop I was usually shaken out of my nightmare by Uncle Birillo, his mustache secured by a strip of Elastoplast, or I was smothered out of it by Aunt Ninfa's bosom scented with verbena, into which I was plunged. If I was particularly unlucky, and Signora Pucillo got to me first, I could expect to be pinched awake by her arthritic fingers, and in the light from the passage my first glimpse of reality would be the far from reassuring sight of a face like thunder, minus its teeth, framed by an enormous nightcap of pea-green gauze. Throughout the rumpus, Fiamma snored and snorted undisturbed.

When I attended the outpatients' clinic at the psychiatry unit on Tuesdays and Thursdays, Dr. Boncoddo listened with only half an ear to my problems, and before long I began to fear the repetitive nature of my trauma and my nightmares was boring him. I did my best to invent variations, but even then he showed little interest.

One Thursday, before I had even launched into a new and entirely fictitious range of fears and desires that I had prepared earlier, I noticed the doctor was crying. When I asked what was troubling him, it was as though a mighty dam was bursting open. The strain of listening to other people's troubles all day at work, coupled with an unhappy home life, was bringing him close to the edge.

He suspected his lover, Nicodemo, of having an affair with the lascivious butcher Fontanelli; Nicodemo's high-spending ways had left him in debt up to his eyebrows; his mother was sick; his moped had been stolen that morning; he was brutally overworked; and his head of department, Dr. Farranda, was a tyrant who didn't understand him. Because of all the stress, he had developed an unsightly rash, his hair was falling out, and in addition, his libido was suffering.

After this I felt an enormous sense of relief that I didn't have to entertain Dr. Boncoddo anymore, and during our sessions I listened to him in silence, merely nodding my head from time to time, absorbing all he could tell me like a sponge. Although I was only sixteen, I gained a lot of knowledge about life, which I felt could only benefit me in future. More important, from this I learned that psychiatry couldn't help me get over Mamma's death: deep down I knew that the only person I could rely on for help was myself.

By the time I reached this conclusion, it was already Christmas, our first Christmas without Mama. Faded paper chains went up in physiotherapy, and Drusilla Morelli began wearing a pair of joke reindeer antlers. In psychiatry, the atmosphere grew ever more frosty as the annual departmental party approached, which, according to Dr. Boncoddo, was always a bloodbath. While we weren't expecting much of a celebration at the Via Gregorio, none of us could have predicted just how miserable it was going to be.

The precious crib figures we had collected since we were tiny had been lost in the move from the Via Giulia, and it couldn't be Christmas without them. Uncle Birillo tried to make us feel better by blowing up a few balloons, but his asthma prevented him from giving them the necessary firmness, without which they were sad and shrunken, the texture of shriveled grapes.

I couldn't stop thinking about our usual Christmas with Mamma: the party at the Magnolia club for which we always had a new dress. It was a rare treat watching Mamma perform, and every time, I felt the thrill of seeing her up on the stage under the bright lights, where she seemed a glamorous stranger, not our own familiar Mamma. This impression was reinforced when she sang those Bing Crosby numbers—"White Christmas," "Jingle Bells," and "Rudolph the Red-Nosed Reindeer"—in heavily accented English, a language she didn't understand. Then how the audience would applaud! And later, Signor Saltini would shower us with expensive gifts and send us home in his limousine. Our little kitchen would be filled with pomegranates, marzipan cherubs, fig-filled cookies, hazelnut brittle, dried fruits, and the scent of roasting chestnuts, and Mamma would make special *castagnaccio*, which we distributed among our neighbors. We went to mass, and then to the fairground; we played *tombola,* danced to the music on the gramophone, and in the evening, out of a sense of duty, we paid a visit to Uncle Birillo and Aunt Ninfa.

This year, Aunt Ninfa, for some mysterious reason, was in a thunderous mood throughout the holiday. She refused to speak to Uncle Birillo, or to listen to him, and made the rest of us pass messages between them, even when they were in the same room.

"Freda, inform your uncle I need a kilo of the good tripe from Tripoto, and a bag of sugared almonds."

"Fiamma, remind your uncle to pay the tip to the bread boy—the small one with the swellings—and the street sweeper."

Then, having issued her instructions, Aunt Ninfa would

retreat into the kitchen, slamming the door shut behind her, only to reappear immediately, like a figure from a Swiss clock. Not surprisingly, all the Christmas baking she did in her fury turned out bad. The *pangiallo* of candied fruits, nuts, raisins, and almond paste was a leaden thing that shattered the plate of Signora Pucillo's false teeth. As the dentist didn't reopen until after Epiphany, the signora was reduced to having her food mashed like a baby's, which didn't improve her own sour temper. The *maiale porchettato* Aunt Ninfa prepared poisoned Fiamma and Uncle Birillo, and the overcrowded apartment was soon filled with the sound of violent vomiting. Thankfully I wasn't affected: then, as now, I had a cast-iron stomach.

Despite my heavy hints over previous weeks, my parrot did not materialize, and I was livid. Mamma had promised me a parrot, and the patchwork cushion, pixie hat, and small spiny cactus provided by my uncle and aunt were not, in my view, a suitable substitute. I tossed them out of the window, and they landed on the head of a passing priest.

It was a relief to us all when the holidays were over, and Uncle Birillo and Fiamma were able to stop vomiting and return to work. Aunt Ninfa stopped being furious, and became instead tearful. She assumed the mantle of a martyr and consumed vast quantities of marzipan fruits. At least now she was able to resume her daily visits to her hairdresser, Raffaello, whom she regarded as a sage, slavishly following his whimsical and often contradictory advice. Signora Pucillo was able to have her false teeth fixed, and return to her senior citizens luncheon club, where she continued to vie with the trollop Telma Maccarrone for the attentions of the club's sprightly chairman, Signor Felice.

The start of the new year, 1966, was a cathartic one for me, and I resolved to take control of my own life as much as I could. I did not return to the hospital, and gave away my crutches to a lame beggar with too many fingers on his right hand. My neck, leg, and skull were virtually restored, and it was time for Drusilla Morelli to find herself a new victim. I knew Dr. Boncoddo needed me, but didn't want him to become too dependent upon me: in the end he would see it was for the best.

I thwarted Uncle Birillo's plans to send me back to school, and Aunt Ninfa's scheme for me to become an apprentice to her hairdresser. Instead, I took myself to see Signora Dorotea Pompi at her funeral parlor in the Vicolo Sugarelli.

five

Signora Pompi hadn't forgotten me. In fact she threw her arms around me and marveled at the success and speed of my recovery. I told her I wanted to become an embalmer, and she was delighted to take me on as her trainee. It transpired that she had been advertising for a junior in the labor exchange for several weeks, but apart from one pimpled youth who listed his hobby on the application form as necrophilia, she had received no interest at all.

I couldn't have chosen a more prestigious establishment to pursue my calling. The signora's family had been undertakers and embalmers for countless generations. Not only had they interred every pope since Gregory the Great, but, the signora confided to me, they had even embalmed Saint Peter himself.

She began by showing me around her premises. Beyond the entrance hall—where Calipso Longo, the motherly receptionist, greeted the bereaved—were two chapels of rest, the staff room, and the office. Behind was the yard, where the private ambulance was kept, and in the back was the stockroom containing the coffins and other supplies, the cold storage area where the bodies reposed in drawers like those of a big filing cabinet, and adjoining it was the embalming suite where I was to work.

It was a light room lined with white tiles and smelled of the geranium disinfectant Aunt Ninfa endorsed. On either side there was a sloping metal table with a sink at its foot, and rubber hoses wound neatly in coils were fixed to the walls. There was a trolley with rows of surgical implements arranged on it, and between the tables was a bank of giant containers filled with bright pink fluid.

We put on green overalls—I borrowed one of the signora's, which swamped me (soon I would have my very own ones with my name embroidered in black letters over the breast pocket, "Freda Castro") and white rubber boots (fortunately our feet were the same size). Then we wheeled Signora Fortuna out of refrigeration and slid her onto the metal table.

She had died the previous day of natural causes—in fact, according to her date of birth, Signora Fortuna was one hundred and eleven years old—and to me she looked just as if she were asleep. Except, of course, that she was too still and too quiet, and her tiny body had no living presence anymore. She was like a very old, shrunken, wrinkled, and slightly balding doll.

We removed Signora Fortuna's nightgown, and sponged her down with germicide. She looked very vulnerable, lying there naked, and I felt a bit embarrassed for her, but I hoped she knew she was in safe hands.

I didn't feel the least bit squeamish—indeed I was fascinated—as Signora Pompi explained everything to me as she went along. First she took a scalpel and made incisions on the right side of Signora Fortuna's neck: in the carotid artery and the jugular vein. Then she inserted two tubes—one to pump in the embalming fluid—and the other to allow the blood gathered inside the body to drain out.

As I watched I could see the veins plumping up with the pink fluid, giving Signora Fortuna a healthy rosiness in place of her former pallor. When the veins in her baby feet started to swell, we knew we had inserted enough fluid, and stopped the pump. At the same time, the blood flowed out from the other tube and was collected in a drum for disposal.

Then Signora Pompi stitched up the incisions she had

made with the precision of a surgeon, and also put a stitch in Signora Fortuna's mouth to keep it closed.

"It's very important to get the lips to meet naturally," she said. "We can't have her scowling at the relatives."

The next step was to give her a thorough wash with soapy water, clean her fingernails, and shampoo her hair. Signora Pompi allowed me to blow-dry it, and I did my best to fluff it up and make it look like it did in the photograph the family had given us, although I think a lot of it had fallen out since the picture was taken.

Then we dressed Signora Fortuna in her winter underwear, stockings, and her tiny wedding dress—yellowed now with age—and the satin slippers she had last worn as a bride, back in 1872.

Finally Signora Pompi made up her face with special mortuary cosmetics—powder, rouge, and lipstick, taking care to make her look as lifelike as possible.

"I'd say she doesn't look a day over seventy-five," said Signora Pompi with pride, standing back to admire the effect of her work. And I have to say I think Signora Fortuna looked even better dead than she had alive.

At last she was ready to be placed in the deluxe *Ultima Cena* coffin her sons had selected, the final adjustments were made, and she was wheeled through to the chapel of rest to receive visits from her relatives and friends.

I was so impressed with Signora Pompi that I wanted to be the best pupil she could ever have, and hoped in time to make her really proud of me. On my way back to the Via Gregorio that evening I stopped off at the public library and took out all the books on embalming I could find. I was exhilarated. I had had such a good day, and was so pleased with myself at having found my true calling so early in life.

Unfortunately my delight in my newfound career didn't extend to my uncle and aunt and to Signora Pucillo.

"You're going to do what?" the three of them chorused when I got back to the apartment, trying to be unobtrusive.

I looked round for Fiamma for moral support, but she wasn't there. That evening she had gone to the cinema with Signor Cremoso, the man who sold *gelati* from a kiosk in the Piazza di Spagna all summer long. This being the dead of winter, he was obliged to offer his services as a relief floor buffer to the Ministry, which was where Fiamma met him.

Influenced more than she would admit by Mamma's prediction for her future, Fiamma was determined to date only fools. Spurning anyone with a claim to good sense, like poor Ruperto, who still passed the nights sighing under our window, she homed in on those who showed signs of stupidity.

Fiamma was attracted by the way Signor Cremoso's lower jaw stuck way out in front of his upper one, like one of those model Neanderthals they have in the Natural History Museum. All too often she confused ugliness with stupidity. In the case of the ice-cream salesman, she found both. As well as his elongated skull, he possessed only one tooth, although I have to say it was a good big one, which he displayed proudly at the front of his mouth.

The date began well enough. Cremoso bought Fiamma the popcorn she craved, and although he couldn't share it with her, he satisfied himself with a cornet of an inferior artificial vanilla. The movie was good too. *Thunderball,* which had just come out—one of those James Bond adventures Fiamma loved.

Afterward Cremoso walked Fiamma home, and thought about trying to hold her hand. Although he had offered a taxi ride—the equivalent of a whole day's buffing—Fiamma wasn't yet ready to put her trust in a motor vehicle. The good-night kiss, delivered in full view of the lovelorn Ruperto, lurking outside as usual, sealed the fate of this promising affair.

Trembling and feverish, the ice-cream man puckered up and leaned forward. Quite how it happened, nobody knows, but the lone tooth, itself eager to play a part, bit clean through

Fiamma's upper lip. Fiamma's scream sliced through the night, bringing everybody in the surrounding buildings down into the street.

The blood loss was terrible. Lips enjoy a good bleed, and Fiamma's, smeared inexpertly with "Coral Whisper," was no exception. Blood gushed onto the sidewalk forming a stain that is there still, and can be viewed by those with an interest in that sort of thing, just to the left of the stone steps, outside number three hundred and thirty-eight.

Fortunately for Fiamma, Ruperto was at the ready with his medical expertise and quickly stemmed the flow of blood with a swab, treated the wound with antiseptic cream, and patched it with Elastoplast, all of which he carried in his pockets in anticipation of just such an emergency as this.

He got no thanks from Fiamma. Cremoso stood forlornly by, knowing that the tooth had blown it for him (if this happened again, he would have to think seriously about having it removed; although it was the last one, he couldn't afford to be sentimental). Uncle Birillo looked askance at the culprit, and asked Fiamma whether his behavior warranted a beating, but she dismissed the suggestion with a wave of her hand. She retreated magnificently into the building without giving Ruperto, who had saved her life, a second glance.

Aunt Ninfa felt bad for the youth, and invited him in for

a cup of coffee, as it was a cold night, and already he had been standing there for some hours, but Ruperto declined. He knew that his appearance in the apartment would infuriate Fiamma, and he couldn't risk her hating him any more than she did already. And so we left him there, with the chill rising up through the thin soles of his shoes, and came inside to the warmth of the parlor, brightly lit, toasting chestnuts in the stove, and sipping steaming cups of hot sweet milk flavored with cinnamon.

Despite the opposition of my uncle and aunt, Signora Pucillo, and also of Fiamma, who objected to the smell of formaldehyde that followed me around and infiltrated our bedroom, I continued my training with Signora Dorotea (as I came to call her), and the two years that followed I devoted to learning my art in its every aspect. I was a natural, so Signora Dorotea noted with joy, and after gaining a distinction in my diploma from the School of Morticians, I embarked on an advanced course in "Trauma."

Acceptance from my relatives did not come until April 17, 1968, which was Signora Pucillo's ninetieth birthday, and the day on which she chose to die. There had been an afternoon of bridge, as usual, and Signora Pucillo and Signor Felice had been doing so well that success went quite to their heads, and during one of the rubbers the dapper signor took the liberty of placing his hand on Signora Pucillo's thigh beneath the table. Although nothing was said, she felt like a girl again.

Aunt Ninfa had prepared a tea and had even baked a cake with pink icing, and there were gifts too: two packs of pristine playing cards, linen handkerchiefs, a posy of lilacs, and a beaded change purse. The best present of all came from Signor Felice. Wrapped in a sheet of paper on which he had drawn a love heart with a shaky hand, was a tiny silver birdcage, inside which were two miniature songbirds with foliage of red enamel.

Signora Pucillo's happiness was complete. Once the guests had departed, she sat down in her chair in the parlor, and without saying a word to anyone, she removed her spectacles and died.

A tearful Aunt Ninfa rang me at work, and within minutes Signor Porzio and I were on our way to Aurelio with a superior casket of mountain ash in the rear of the ambulance. The following day, in the chapel of rest, Signora Pucillo was unveiled, her beauty in death leading all who saw her to forget her plainness in life.

Signor Felice was disconsolate. Why hadn't he married her forty years ago, when she was a fresh, youthful widow, and he a man in the prime of life with full control over his bowel movements and a willing member? Why had he wasted so much time? Now he had lost his chance. Oh, he couldn't bear it!

Signora Dorotea kindly bent the rules and allowed him to stay overnight in the chapel, where the body gave off the scent of jasmine, and he spent those few precious hours gazing at his beloved, describing in detail the life they would have had together if he only hadn't been so stupid.

Then at last Aunt Ninfa and Uncle Birillo understood my calling, and I like to think they were as proud of me as they were of Fiamma.

My sister surprised us all by bringing to the funeral reception a young man we had not set eyes on before. Aunt Ninfa was pleased to note he had a full set of teeth, but nevertheless the signs did not augur well. Aside from the fact that his loud suit and comedy tie did not show the respect necessary at a funeral, and his wolfing consumption of the pink birthday cake, which was being handed round, betrayed a lack of good manners, it was his conversation that set him apart from all sensible people. His tasteless jokes, his insistence on performing magic tricks, and his braying laugh were all preferable to his monologues on fish or types of pickle. All the while, Fiamma watched our reactions to him with a blinkless eye and a smile playing upon her lips.

When all the guests had gone, including the dreadful young man, and we were washing up the cups and plates and tidying the parlor, casually Fiamma voiced her intention of marrying him.

"But he's a perfect fool!" gasped Uncle Birillo, aghast.

Fiamma's eyes gleamed with satisfaction.

"So much the better," she replied.

In the years after the accident, Fiamma worked her way up from the puppy farm to the middle rungs at the Ministry. At the same time, in the field of her love life, she worked her way down from Signor Cremoso.

In those days, at the Ministry, there were far fewer women than there are now, and Fiamma was something of a novelty. She had her pick of a great many young men who were impressed by her beauty and by her meteoric rise, and I have to say, Fiamma left no stone unturned in her search for a nincompoop.

Since the ice-cream incident she had tried to conduct her affairs in private, but I know she had dozens of liaisons, the details of which she logged with her customary clinical precision in a leather-bound volume she kept beneath her pillow.

When she was out, I read it. Here is a sample of what details she recorded under each heading. This is one entry dated March 23, 1966:

CONTESTANT: Miseno Numitore
CATEGORY: Under Filing Clerk, P-S Section
DATE: walk in the Giardino del Quirinale, coffee in the Piazza Barberini
CONVERSATION: dull but sensible
HANDS: often wet and trembling
KISSES: salival
OVERALL VERDICT: insufficiently stupid

However, in an entry dated April 17, 1968, the same day as Signora Pucillo's birth and death, I read with interest the following:

CONTESTANT: Polibio Naso
CATEGORY: Tea Boy, Investigations Section
DATE: Pickle Factory in Via Flaminia
CONVERSATION: completely moronic
HANDS: dry, firm, wandering

KISSES: magic!

OVERALL VERDICT: promising

ACTION REQUIRED: follow-up date with a view to marriage

This was in fact the last entry in the journal. On the following day Fiamma dispensed with her grid squares and had simply scrawled across the page: *Polibio Naso is the perfect fool. Action required: marry him.*

And so she did. On the day of the wedding, which followed rapidly after the funeral, Fiamma remained irritatingly cheerful, although Uncle Birillo, Aunt Ninfa, and I were horrified to see her throwing herself away. But I knew what nobody else did: she was assuaging her guilt over the accident by making Mamma's prediction for her come true.

On the same day that Fiamma packed her clothes for her honeymoon, and her other possessions for her married life in the Via della Lupa, I too packed my bags.

I was nearly nineteen now, and was taking my own apartment. Although it was unusual in those days for a single girl to live alone, I was old beyond my years, and wanted my independence. Uncle Birillo felt depressed at the thought that he had failed us, but, like Fiamma, I was determined to go my own way, and there was nothing he could do to stop me.

And so Fiamma married Polibio in a magnificent ceremony at Santa Maria Maddalena—she wasn't about to do the thing by halves—and as she walked up the aisle, I noticed that she had artificially reddened the scar on her forehead so it stood out like a stigmata.

At the back stood Ruperto, the medical student, the man Fiamma should have married. He was dry-eyed and pale-faced, and had the look of a man for whom life had become a baffling charade. Those who knew him were troubled by his air of calm desperation, and were fully aware that he was poised on the brink of disaster.

As the newlyweds drove off in a pony chaise and a blizzard of confetti, Ruperto watched from the corner on the opposite side of the street, where the plane tree was marked with a little wooden cross in memory of a murder, and where the manhole cover was corroded and in need of attention.

As Ruperto plummeted through the rusty grating to meet his filthy death in the cavernous labyrinth of sewers that riddled the city, his only thought was of Fiamma, who had ceased to recall his very existence.

Early the following morning I embraced my uncle and aunt, and taking all my possessions in a small cardboard box, I set off for my new life in my own apartment.

"Won't you take a few pork cheeks with you, Freda?" Blubbered Aunt Ninfa, tears streaming down her fat face.

"No, really, there'll be food where I'm going," I said, making for the door.

"A little *pecorino* at least? Some artichokes? I'll pack them right up."

"Honestly, I'll be fine."

"Birillo," she bellowed, "why don't you say something?"

"Ninfa," he spat as though her name tasted bad, "how many times have I told you not to shout in my ears?

What do you want me to say? She doesn't need any artichokes . . ."

I slipped away as the two squared up to one another like wrestlers in a ring. I knew it would be a short time before the rumpus grew ugly and a longer time before they realized I had gone. As I climbed on a bus bound for the Centro Storico, I could still hear the wailing of Aunt Ninfa, which carried right along the block, above the roar of the traffic and the hooting of horns.

My apartment was in the Via dei Cappellari, one of the narrow alleyways leading off the Campo dei Fiori, just a few streets away from the Via Giulia, where I had grown up. Immediately I had the feeling I was coming home.

I threw open the windows to air the place, and soon my rooms were full of the succulent aroma of baking bread, coming from the *forno* opposite. The laundry strung on lines between the buildings fluttered like brightly colored flags welcoming me. From behind the neighboring shutters I could hear gossip, laughter, the radio news. Somewhere a baby was crying, and Sam Cook was singing "What a Wonderful World," accompanied by the clattering of pots and pans. Below, the street sweeper was trundling his cart, children were playing, pigeons were pecking, and stray dogs were sniffing, all of them scattered from time to time by the passage of speeding scooters.

I was thrilled with it all. I was independent. And I was about to do something I had longed to for ages: I was going to acquire the parrot for which I had become unbearably broody. Yes, in the Via Gregorio there had always been some lame reason for thwarting me: Uncle Birillo's asthma, Signora Pucillo's phobias, Aunt Ninfa's hairdresser's disapproval, Fiamma's refusal to allow a birdcage into our bedroom. Now I could do as I liked, and relishing my newfound freedom, I set out once more.

In the livestock market in the Via Ponderosa all kinds of animals were offered for sale. Goats, cows, pigs, sheep, rabbits, and mules were lined up in pens next to the truck park, and the air was rich with the fug of their warm bodies, and of steaming dung, which local children stole for their mothers to put on their roses. The sound of chomping and snorting vied with the din of the bartering merchants, the hooting of horns, and the drone of diesel engines.

Beyond was a pavilion where more exotic creatures were occasionally displayed, and I'm sure that even at that time trade in many of them must have been illegal. There were gibbons and sometimes even gorillas brought into the docks by sailors, enormous pythons, poisonous tarantulas, iguanas, wild cats baring glistening fangs, as well as brown bears and armadillos.

I made my way through the crowds of hawkers and pickpockets to the Alley of the Birds. From the sound of squawking, cooing, shrieking, piping, singing, and chattering, you could imagine yourself in a tropical rain forest, rather than a passageway in Roma. Beneath my feet the ground was sticky from the litter of squashed guavas and earthworms, plums and peaches, pine kernels, walnuts, and the remains of the mice fed to the vultures.

Among enclosures containing penguins and peacocks, I found an ornate gilt cage containing a tiny baby parrot with the brightest turquoise feathers. His head was tucked under his wing as though he was hiding from the world, and I knew then I had found the parrot destined for me.

"He doesn't talk," said a wise old mynah bird perched on a cash register nearby.

"I don't mind," I said. "I'll take him anyway."

I paid the mynah bird what he asked for—I couldn't tell whether he was the proprietor of the stall or whether he was just looking after it for someone else. The price seemed reasonable, and included the cage and a packet of seed. I called the little parrot Pierino, and proudly I carried him back to my apartment. Once released, he began flying around making white dots on my limited furnishings, and squawking with what I like to think was happiness.

After a week Fiamma returned from her honeymoon journey to Sabaudia. In her absence Aunt Ninfa had confidently prepared our old room to receive her, and had tentatively inquired of her priest about the process of annulment. She and my uncle were convinced Fiamma would by now be regretting her mistake, and they would be there to help her pick up the pieces.

Yet to all our surprise, Fiamma returned radiant with happiness, and with a gleam in her eye that was a mystery to me at that time.

The newlyweds appeared at the apartment in the Via Gregorio for the traditional first visit, during which they were unable to restrain themselves and act decently, in fact, they couldn't keep their hands off each other. Aunt Ninfa hadn't predicted this. She had been so sure of a separation that she hadn't bothered to get anything in for the tea that custom demanded, and there was an embarrassing interlude while she blundered about borrowing the necessary sweetmeats from the neighbors.

"It won't last," she brayed when the turtledoves could bear it no longer, and had flown back to their love nest in the Via della Lupa. But in this my aunt was destined to be completely wrong and horribly disappointed.

My nineteenth birthday arrived—which, of course, I didn't celebrate—apart from my usual visit to Mamma's grave. I told Mamma what little news I had since the previous week, which mainly concerned Pierino (I was as proud as a new mother), and an interesting challenge at work (a case of severe lupus—very difficult to disguise).

Anyway, I arranged the forget-me-nots in a flask of water, and had just dusted off the headstone when the sexton (the cheerful chubby one, not the tall one with the squint), who had been lurking for some time, approached me and asked if I would like to see his birthmark.

Now, I had seen a great many birthmarks in my time, but I didn't want to seem ungrateful for his offer, so I followed him across the cemetery to the little hut where he kept his picks and shovels, some fallen angels, and a large jar of licorice sticks. It transpired he didn't have a birthmark after all—at least not that I saw.

Still, when he had shown me what he wanted me to see, I thanked him, and we parted on cordial terms: he to ring the vesper bell, and me to eat an ice cream—two scoops of pistachio and one of lemon.

Shortly after this incident, although I don't think it was related in any way, I came out in a rash of green spots, and felt an itching deep inside me that I couldn't scratch.

I showed the spots to Signora Dorotea, worried that I had caught some sort of disease from one of the corpses. The summer was already unusually hot, and many of them had boils and rich varieties of creeping fungus.

"The remedy is simple," she said. "You need a man, Freda Castro. It's only natural, and nothing to be ashamed of."

Perhaps she was right, but in my job I didn't come in contact with many members of the opposite sex, at least not live ones. Still, that same day I was surprised when Cuniberto Moretti (one of the relief pallbearers, who was at other times a vendor of vanilla pods), sidled up to me in the staff room where I was rubbing some balsam into my pustules and asked me out on a date. Thinking about it afterward, I was sure Signora Dorotea must have put him up to it.

I certainly didn't want to go out with him. I didn't feel attracted to him in any way. Some girls, I'm sure, would have been drawn to his brown-tinged teeth, and the way clumps of hair sprouted from his neck, but I wasn't one of them. Still, I felt bad about saying no, so, reluctantly I agreed.

That evening, Cuniberto was loitering in the yard as I returned Signor Giordano to his drawer in cold storage and locked up. He had acquired a bunch of tired-looking daisies, which he thrust at me, blushing.

Together we walked the short distance to Fargo's, where we shared the empty premises with a sullen waiter who had long given up his struggle with personal hygiene and an energetic bluebottle who managed to be everywhere at once. I was grateful to the fly. At least it saved us from the silence there would otherwise have been.

Lemonade was ordered and banged down on the Formica tabletop with a force that ensured much of it was spilled. What was left we sipped in between stilted attempts at conversation. Really, there was nothing to say. After fifteen minutes that seemed as long as a week I stood up to leave. Cuniberto seemed surprised.

"Don't you want those?" he asked, motioning toward the daisies on the counter; they had wilted and were giving off a pungent odor of decay. I shook my head.

Outside he surprised me by lunging at me with his lips, teeth, and tongue in quick succession. I didn't understand why. Perhaps he thought it was expected of him. I thanked him and set off alone for my apartment.

That night, as I inserted my fingers between those folds of flesh that seemed to harbor the itchiest of the itchy places, I thought, if that was dating, I could do without it.

ten

Yet despite this inauspicious beginning, between then and the summer of 1971, I did have my share of flirtations. Not on the same scale as Fiamma, of course, because she was as brazen as I was bashful, but I tried to find out about love, and with nobody to guide me, I felt like the one wearing the blindfold in a game of blindman's bluff.

Signora Dorotea put her faith in sales representatives. She was always making appointments for me to see one or another, even when we had no intention of buying what they were selling. Mostly they were purveyors of rubber gloves, embalming fluids, descalents, powders, waxes, prostheses, cosmetics, wigs, or false teeth. Almost always, of course, they were elderly and liver-spotted, but occasionally a youngish one appeared, struggling beneath the weight of his suitcase of samples. Then Signora Dorotea would nod and wink, and drop the heaviest of hints, which usually had the effect of sending him running to the door.

Another strand of her strategy was to send me on every seminar, training course, and trade show she could find. I became a regular on the circuit, but despite Signora Dorotea's coaching in small talk, I still found it difficult to overcome my shyness. I just couldn't think of anything to say to the funeral directors, professional mourners, specialist embalmers, coffin makers, and stone masons I encountered at these events.

Ernesto Porcino was the most promising of the lot, and although Signora Dorotea didn't consider him good enough for me, she wouldn't pour scorn on what she regarded as her only, albeit slim, chance of a wedding. We first met at an exposition of false eyeballs, where he was demonstrating a new line he had personally developed: eyes that were actually able to produce their own tears. They caused a sensation. As well as ordering a consignment that would last us for a decade, I accepted when Signor Porcino asked me to accompany him to the after-show party. I had never been to a party before. I was dazzled by the Signor's verbosity. He did enough talking for both of us, even answering on my behalf the questions he had put to me. For the first time in my dealings with the opposite sex, I didn't feel handicapped by my conversational inadequacy.

Ernesto (as I shall call him from now on) was more mature than the previous young men I had met. In fact, he was forty-five to my twenty-two, and had the accompanying hairlessness, bunions, sweats, cramps, and obesity, but I wasn't looking for film-star good looks; I was looking for a ventriloquist.

Despite the fact that he was unable to throw his voice (he did try, but failed miserably), we soon got to the taking-off-our-clothes stage at Ernesto's instigation. Although it went no further, I was mesmerized by his thing, which was only just visible behind the overhanging bulk of his belly. And on those occasions when he allowed me to cushion it in the palm of my hand, I was delighted at the way it transformed from a pale and unobtrusive pink to a throbbing shaft of angry purple. Those furtive encounters took place once beneath the umbrella pines in the Valle d'Inferno, and once in the chapel of rest at the funeral parlor when Signora Dorotea and Signor Porzio were visiting with her married sister, Loretta, at Punta Ala.

Delighted as I was by Ernesto's willy, and feeling that I was on the cusp of some secret and mysterious awakening, I was anxious to do more than merely hold it in my hand.

Ernesto was touched, I could tell, by my youthful ardor, and racked his brains to come up with a solution, but his lodgings, he told me, were in the house of elderly virgins in a perilous state of health, and the presence of a nubile temptress in his apartment would be enough to propel at least one, if not two, or even all three of them, into a tragic decline.

I was thrilled to hear myself described as a nubile temptress, and throwing caution to the wind, I invited him for the assignation to my own rooms in the Via dei Cappellari. Flushed with expectation and delight, I opened the door to admit him, aware that Signor Tontini was spying on me from the stairs.

Immediately Ernesto rushed to the bathroom—he had been on the road with his samples all day, he said, and was bursting for a pee. Shortly afterward he reemerged, wearing nothing but a long blond wig and brandishing a wand.

This was the moment Pierino had been waiting for. He sliced across the room in a motion that was invisible it was so fast, and set upon, with his sharp beak, the tempting parts of my would-be lover.

Ernesto's screams rent the air, and his flesh was ripped to pieces before I could persuade Pierino to end his attack, and tempt him back into his cage with the promise of a ripe and juicy fig.

I was sorry the affair had ended in this way, before I had experienced the full fascination of the purple probe, now limp, and bruised, and bleeding; but I knew that if Pierino hated Ernesto, which he clearly did, then there was no way I could allow things to develop further.

Aside from his pain, which must have been agonizing, my false-eye maker was livid. To my surprise, but I must admit also to my satisfaction, it transpired that the three virgin octogenarian landladies were a figment of his imagination. What prevented him from allowing me into his home happened to be, in fact, Signora Porcino, and the five Porcini. The signora was possessed of a jealous streak, and this was his very final last chance. How he was going to explain away his injuries, he simply didn't know.

He dressed quickly, and I pushed him gently out onto the landing and shut the door. With his powers of storytelling I was confident he would be able to think of something.

I experienced no amorous encounters for a while after this and, indeed, was beginning to come to the premature but nonetheless accurate conclusion that sex was more trouble than it was worth, when I won a prize in a contest that changed the course of my life.

eleven

I kept abreast of Ernesto's progress with his weeping eyes in a trade periodical we received at work, *Mortician's Monthly*, and felt no small degree of pride when I saw the photographs of him demonstrating them at such far-flung shows as Tel Aviv and Bombay.

Signora Dorotea, to whom I confessed everything, was outraged by his perfidy, and whenever she saw his picture, made dark mutterings about what she would do to him given the chance. But my recollection of what lay beneath the ill-fitting salesman's suit filled me with nostalgia.

Then, in the March issue of 1972, which bore the enticing headline, "Live Man Buried in Shocking Blunder," there was a competition for readers to win a luxury cruise to Egypt, to explore the mysteries of the pharaohs, the pyramids, and the Sphinx. Signora Dorotea became overexcited and insisted that I enter.

"I know you'll win it," she said, "and the man of your dreams."

I can't even remember what the questions were now, but they were easy enough, and my answers were, "one liter," "wax," "rigor mortis," and "decomposition." With the last part I had more difficulty. I had to write a sentence of no more than twelve words explaining why I deserved to win the cruise. I hemmed and hawed over this one. It was the word "deserved" that I found particularly tricky. I didn't feel I deserved anything. I showed my various attempts to Signora Dorotea, who snorted with derision,

"You'll never win if you put that," she said.

Then, finally losing patience, she instructed,

"Freda, write this," then dictated, "I love *Mortician's Monthly* and share it with all my friends."

"But it isn't true," I complained. "I would never give this magazine to anybody." However, history was set to prove me a liar.

"Never say never, Freda," she said, and snatching the coupon from me, mailed it.

Then we waited.

On the closing date, as I was trimming Signor Settebello's

mustache, which had grown bushy since his death, I received a phone call.

"What did I tell you?" screamed Signora Dorotea, lifting me off my feet in a bear hug. "I just knew you would win!"

From there things moved fast. Immediately a truckload of promotional products appeared, together with the contest organizer, a photographer, a stylist, and two assistants. I was required to pose in the cold room surrounded by giant bottles of solution proudly displaying the label of the sponsor, Dricol.

I appeared on the cover in the May issue. It wasn't a bad photo, although I wish I hadn't agreed to expose quite so much of my legs. Inside there was a wildly exaggerated biography of the lucky winner, along with equally exaggerated praise for the product. I know because we wouldn't use it. It turned the flesh of the corpses an unattractive greenish color, as if they were seasick, and the smoke it gave off was poisonous.

Nevertheless I felt proud. I was pleased with the thought that Ernesto, wherever he was now, be it Bangkok or Buenos Aires, would see my image splashed on the front cover and would feel the unbearable regret of knowing he had lost me forever.

Signora Dorotea was over the moon, and convinced herself she had become clairvoyant. She immediately sent Signor

Porzio out to get the magazine cover framed, and then she displayed it proudly in the reception area where all the bereaved marveled over it.

I bought several extra copies and gave one to Uncle Birillo and Aunt Ninfa. I had signed my name across it like an autograph. They were so proud. In those days they hadn't got their own phone, so Aunt Ninfa went to the post office with her address book and a stack of coins, and spent all day on the public telephone informing everyone she knew. Soon a line of people wanting to use the phone stretched around the block, furious at Aunt Ninfa's refusal to relinquish the receiver and vacate the kiosk. Uncle Birillo was equally pleased, and congratulated himself on having guided me into the business in the first place.

I gave another copy to Fiamma.

"Is that you?" she asked unnecessarily, and then laughed.

The last copy I gave to Pierino. He dragged it onto the floor of his cage and then shat on it.

twelve

On Thursday June 15, 1972, I was to present myself at Civitavecchia, Banchina 5, where I would, according to the brochure I had been sent, board the *Santa Domenica,* and in so doing, step back into a lost world of luxury and refinement. But I had a lot to do first. Fiamma, who was now pregnant, came round and cast a critical eye over the contents of my wardrobe.

"You can't wear any of this stuff," she said dismissively; "although I suppose if you have to perform any burials at sea, it would be all right."

It was true that most of my clothes had been bought with funerals in mind. In my line of work I could hardly get away with the miniskirts in psychedelic colors and platform shoes in which Fiamma scandalized, but also excited, the grandees at the Ministry.

Together we hit the streets around the Piazza di Spangna, where the sidewalks heaved with shoppers, foreign tourists, ice-cream vendors, gigolos, artists, and priests, and where the very trendiest boutiques in the whole of the city were to be found. Brushing aside my protests, Fiamma quickly filled a suitcase with the flimsiest, shortest, tightest, and most revealing garments she could uncover.

"For heaven's sake, Freda," she snapped. "You're supposed to be twenty-three not forty-seven. You've been middle-aged your whole life."

This came as something of a shock to me at the time, but thinking about it afterward, I supposed she was right.

So my cruise wear was one problem solved; at least it would be if I could summon the courage to put on the neon pink minidress with matching briefs and peaked cap, the gold lamé catsuit, or the super-flared pants and fringed bra top in lime green nylon. Signora Dorotea was to look after Pierino for me. She was the only one I thought I could trust with him.

There was one other thing I knew I had to do before I left.

For some time now Mamma's teeth had been worrying me. At the end of the day, in that space between waking and sleeping, I thought of Mamma's teeth. In the eye of my mind I could see her smile, and I wanted to restore it to her. Now was the time.

Therefore on Sunday June 11, 1972, I took two buses to the place where Mamma's life was snatched, and mine shattered, seven years ago. I had not been there since. The road didn't seem as long as it had then, or as steep. I started walking from the top, remembering all the details of that day that had seemed forgotten.

The poppies growing along the scrubby verge, the white butterflies, the dust rising, the sun hot on my skin, the wind in my face and my hair, plucking at Mamma's hat, her laughter. An invisible band struck up "Io So Perchè," and Mamma's voice sang along. The wind began to whistle faster. It grew louder in my ears. Fiamma's giant bubble of gum burst. The air became taut and tense as the hulk of the car hurtled out of control and roared toward the old man who was waiting for it to consume him.

I ran. My legs couldn't keep pace with me. I thought I would leave them behind as I threw myself onward, faster, down the hill, my arms flailing. I stumbled. I ran on, and on, hardly aware that the screaming I could hear was coming from me. Finally I reached the bottom, and told my legs to stop, but the momentum carried me on for a dozen more paces. I bent over at the waist, letting my torso flop down and the blood fill my head. I was panting so hard I felt sick, and thought I would bring up my lungs and possibly even my heart. I stayed like that for a while, and then stood up, and walked around slowly.

I found the spot where the car had stopped, and where the old man had lain down and died, but there was nothing to mark the place. Just a gaping, screaming emptiness, and somehow this made it all seem even more pointless. Why had it happened? Why?

The nearby house seemed even more ramshackle now than it had then, although at the time I had paid it no attention. Some windows were boarded up, some broken; one of the shutters had bent its hinge and hung down. I pushed my way through the gate grown stiff without use. The garden, then so beautiful, had given way to ivy and thickets of weeds. Thorns snagged at me as I waded through the growth to reach the palm tree. Startled lizards scattered in streams of shifting light. Propped up against the trunk was a wreath of tacky plastic pansies—Aunt Ninfa's handiwork, no doubt.

Halfway up I found what I was looking for. Mamma's teeth. Embedded. Six of them. Tracing the line of a crescent moon. I pulled from my pocket the pair of pliers I had brought with me, and removed the teeth one by one. When I had them all, I wrapped them carefully in a handkerchief and returned to the city.

Later that day I buried them in Mamma's grave, and the following year there sprouted a fine crop of turnips. Why turnips, I don't know, but I was glad.

thirteen

On Thursday morning, Pierino, with Signora Dorotea, Signor Porzio, Uncle Birillo, Aunt Ninfa, Polibio Naso—Fiamma's husband (Fiamma was in a meeting with the president and was unable to attend)—and an old woman with a motor-controlled hand whom I had never set eyes on before, formed a farewell party on the quayside.

The photographer from *Mortician's Monthly* was there again, snapping away through an enormous telephoto lens, and I felt just like a celebrity. There were balloons and streamers, and the ship's band had assembled on the deck, playing jaunty seafaring numbers to welcome me aboard. I didn't realize until I stepped on the gangplank in my new white platform shoes that I had never been anywhere in my life before, and already I felt horribly homesick. How I wanted to turn round and run away. But it was too late. A handsome man in a smart uniform blew a whistle, troops of sailors began heaving at ropes, the great funnel emitted clouds of dirty black smoke, and a throbbing horn, seemingly located deep in the bowels of the ship, gave out a series of blasts that made me quiver.

Before I knew it the ropes were cast loose, the waters foamed and bubbled up between the side of the ship and the dockside, and we were away. The other cruisers cheered and whooped, and a few halfhearted fireworks were set off by an old sea dog whose burn-scarred face and hands showed he had done this sort of thing before, and not with an unqualified degree of success.

I looked down at the huddle of figures waving at me and picked out the woman with the mechanical hand, which waved urgently, never tiring, and I fancied that above the roar of the engines I could detect the squawking voice of Pierino wishing me bon voyage.

I watched my loved ones retreat into the haze, feeling a huge wave of nostalgia, praying fervently that nothing horrible would happen to me while I was away in the wider world. As usual in my life, I was destined to be disappointed.

fourteen

I spent the first half hour of the voyage exploring the ship. Despite the extravagant claims of the competition organizers, my accommodation was to be a shared internal cabin without facilities, in the third-class portion of the vessel. So much for the lost world of luxury and refinement. A steward conducted me to my cabin, where I found the lower birth already occupied by a flabby girl of indeterminate age named Clodia, who, I was surprised to see, had a mechanical hand. I had never seen one in my life before, and yet now, within the space of ten minutes, I had seen two.

It later transpired that Clodia's mother had been the one who joined my farewell party on the quayside. Her nearsightedness made her unable to perceive anything but blobs at a distance, but her vanity wouldn't allow her to acquire glasses. Thus, and not altogether flatteringly, she had mistaken me for her daughter, and waved at me until her mechanism seized.

Clodia was quick to demonstrate with pride the many features of the hand (it certainly was a top-of-the-line model), but I was slightly worried when she drew up the coverlet to reveal under her bunk an enormous tank of spare petrol. The one disadvantage of the hand was its heavy consumption of gas. My only hope was that she didn't smoke. But all too soon she was lighting up king-size cigarettes of full strength, which filled the tiny cabin with a choking smoke. We didn't even have a porthole.

As Clodia puffed, I unpacked. There wasn't a closet, just a couple of metal hangers on the back of the door. In the confined space, I had to stand in my suitcase in order to unpack it. I was horrified at what I found inside. I hadn't really been paying attention when I had been shopping with Fiamma, but even if I had refused some of the items, she would have bought them anyway. She had always had the upper hand.

I knew I wouldn't be able to wear half these things. They just weren't me at all. I couldn't appear in public dressed like this: everything was tiny, tight, and bright. The cruisers—and more worryingly—the crew, would surely think I was soliciting. As I was examining the flimsy scraps in the light of the bare bulb that lurched with the motion of the ship, I became aware of Clodia's eyes bulging.

"Cor," she said eloquently, "what beautiful things you have. Mother won't let me have anything nice. All I've got is this . . ."

She unzipped her holdall and pulled out a number of sensible Crimplene housedresses in somber colors. Not brilliant by any means, but they would have to do.

"All right," I said as though I were doing her an enormous favor, "I'll swap with you."

Clodia's eyes bulged further.

"For real?" she exclaimed.

"For real," I confirmed.

Quickly we climbed into each other's clothes. She was approximately twice my size, but I tied the belt of the dress tight, and didn't think it looked too bad. At least it was decent, which was more than could be said for the hot pants Clodia had struggled into. There was a degree of stretch, but not enough (these were the days before Lycra, after all), and the fabric, strained into submission, had become obscenely transparent. Below, above, and in fact, all around, rolls of white flesh burst out like Hydra's heads, and writhed for supremacy over their neighbors.

"Fantastic," she said.

I then set off to take a look at the facilities, such as they were, with Clodia waddling behind. The bathroom on our deck was intended for use by all eighteen internal cabins, and a long and desperate line was wriggling through the cramped passage, and this was even before the attack of dysentery broke out.

The third-class dining room was evidently not that featured in the brochure. It was painted a nauseous green and had flourescent strips instead of chandeliers. The gilt wood chairs with pink velvet upholstery were only available to the first-class bottoms; here there were wooden benches like those in school. The air was stale with unpleasant odors: grease, garbage, and greens. Through the back, in the galley kitchen, the unappealing cook was preparing dinner. He rested his eyes momentarily on Clodia in the white hot-pants and then continued slicing desultorily at the slab of tripe under his knife.

Standards rose as we climbed to the higher decks. The second-class passageways were freshly painted and brightly lit. The dining room had windows that looked out onto the glittering sea, and there was waiter service instead of a conveyor belt. However it was on the upper deck where the differences were most marked. There were deep red carpets and velvet drapes, mirrors, chandeliers, and lots of highly polished brass. We pressed our noses to the glass of the captain's restaurant and ogled the crystal goblets, damask table linen, and displays of fresh flowers and fruit.

"Stand aside there," said a voice, and we started guiltily as a man in a uniform and white gloves polished away with a cloth the smear where our noses had been.

We slunk away to marvel at the beauty parlor, the hairdressers, and the shops. There was a boutique selling bikinis and sun hats, a newspaper kiosk, and a souvenir stall offering miniature replicas of the *Santa Domenica,* as well as plug-in Eiffel Towers and brightly painted Russian dolls. There was also a casino, a nightclub, and an Entertainment Room where an exciting new program was soon to be announced.

Clodia was astounded by the magnificence, while the bronzed ladies in halter-neck dresses and the gentlemen in safari suits were equally astonished at the sight of her. Before the steward could eject us, I dragged her out onto the sundeck.

Oh, the water was beautiful! It made you want to plunge straight in. It was the bluest blue I had ever seen, and with the sun shining, each individual crest was tipped with molten gold. As I watched, dolphins arched into the air, and schools of flying fish performed somersaults.

I was relieved when Clodia expressed her desire to try her luck at quoits, and I hurried off alone to find a deck chair.

Already I felt lumbered with her. Casually, but undeniably and horribly, we had become a twosome. Stupidly I felt somehow responsible for her, yet I desperately wanted to shake her off. I didn't want to spend the whole five days of the cruise worrying about her.

I sank back, allowing the canvas to cradle my weight, and closed my eyes. The sea breeze left a film of salt on my lips and ruffled through my hair. The sun warmed my face, and for the first time I felt glad that I had come. Perhaps something good would come of it after all. At least I was having new experiences. I kicked off my shoes and thought about falling asleep.

Then a movement to my right side forced my eyes open. I was incensed to find that out of a row of some fifty empty deck chairs, a small, fat man, dressed in a sailor suit, had chosen to suspend himself in the one immediately next to mine.

For some minutes I watched him adjust himself, thinking that when he felt the weight of my stare he would look at me and then I would scowl at him. But he didn't look. He adjusted. Holding on tight to the wooden arms, he gingerly pushed his bottom backward into the canvas until the backs of his bare and beefy knees were hard up against the frame. Then, immediately undoing all the good work he had done, he stuck his legs out straight in front of him, floundered up and down like a fish, slapped his feet down on the planks of the deck (he was wearing kiddie sandals, the kind that have a T-bar and buckle up at the side; usually in navy blue or red, brown if you're a boy; corrugated rubbery sole; he had the blue ones), then brought his bottom close to the frame at the front and stretched out his back and arms. All the while, the joints of the chair creaked vigorously in protest, and I hoped it would collapse, but it didn't. Then, just when I thought he had settled, he drew in his legs and curled himself up into a ball.

He was clearly some sort of a maniac. Perhaps there was a party of them. I imagined the cruise line would offer special rates to institutions, just to fill any vacant spaces.

Next to him, on the far side, was an enormous black suitcase, almost as big as he was. It looked sinister. The kind of suitcase an ax murderer would use to hide a body in. Although I had no fear of bodies, axes I didn't care for. I shuddered.

I thought about moving, but obstinacy held me back. After all, this was my spot. I was here first. I stopped looking at him, and kept my eyes fixed ahead. That way if he made any sudden movement, I would be ready for him. During this uneasy truce, Clodia ran over crying. It appeared the sea air was playing havoc with the hand's delicate mechanism: twice it had clamped shut without warning, once to the ship's rail, and she had struggled for a long time to release herself and was surprised when I hadn't come over to help. The second time it had locked on to a gentleman's set of metal-plated teeth and there had been a horrible scuffle. She had sustained a number of vicious bites, and was going to ask the ship's doctor for a rabies shot, just in case. She didn't know how she was going to show her face in first class again. Not that she had to worry about the latter, for she had already been banned, and a vivid description had been circulated to all the first-class stewards so they could be on the lookout for her.

As she was so upset, I agreed to go back down to the cabin with her and assist her in applying some oil to the moving parts; besides, I was keen to distance myself from the little fat sailor, who I knew was listening to our conversation with all his ears.

fifteen

That night, after lights-out, as we lay in our bunks, I told Clodia how I had won the cruise in a competition.

"Cor," she said, "I've never won anything."

Then I asked her how she happened to be on the *Santa Domenica*. I was astounded to learn that the trip had been a gift from her mother to celebrate Clodia's fortieth birthday. I'd thought she was younger than me! How had I got myself into the position of acting as a nursemaid to a woman almost twice my age? It was ridiculous. How Fiamma would have laughed.

"I'm amazed you're forty, Clodia," I threw over the edge of my bunk. "You certainly don't look it."

"Aw," she said shyly, "Freda, you say the nicest things."

We lapsed into silence as I plotted my escape. If she was forty, she could take care of herself.

"I'll let you into another little secret"—Clodia's voice came from below—"Mother wanted me to come on the cruise to find a husband, but I don't want to."

"Why not?" I asked idly, not considering her chances of success high anyway.

"Because, silly, I prefer girls."

Things were going from bad to worse. Quickly I made some puffing and snorting noises, hoping she would be fooled into thinking I had fallen suddenly asleep. How would I repel her advances if she stormed my bunk? I prayed that nature wouldn't call in the night. If it did, how could I avoid falling into her clutches?

"Freda, would you like to come down into my bunk?" she called in a soppy voice, trying to sound seductive.

My sleep ploy had failed. Now what was I going to do?

Thankfully a rumpus came to my rescue. There was a terrible commotion out in the passage. Screams rang out as though there were a massacre, and then the sound of a crowd surging through the narrow gangways, shouting, shoving, crashing, banging, more screaming, and scuttling. It was terrifying in the dark. My first thought was that there was a fire.

Or that the ship had been torpedoed. Or that it had foundered on rocks.

Immediately I thought how I would never live to see Pierino and my loved ones ever again. I pictured the moving and majestic funeral Signora Dorotea would give me, although it was unlikely my body would be recovered, and my superior polished coffin would go empty to my grave.

Below, Clodia rummaged for her cigarette lighter, and a feeble gleam illuminated the cabin. (The lights in third class were centrally controlled and were switched off at nine PM sharp; first and second class were not subject to this curfew, and could have their lights on all night long if they wanted). Outside the mayhem continued, growing ever more frenzied, and the stomping of feet, running up and down confused me. Were these people trapped?

"What shall we do?" whispered Clodia.

There was no question in my mind that we should evacuate. If there was a fire, with Clodia's massive deposit of petrol in the cabin, this was the very last place we wanted to be. I pulled the back hem of my nightgown up between my legs, Gandhi-style, and gingerly descended the stepladder. I could feel Clodia's eyes on my thighs.

"Come on!" I ordered her, and wrenched open the door.

As we prepared to join the stampede, there was a sudden rush of fur against my legs. Lots of furry things were running over my bare feet, and the air was filled with a savage squeaking. I began screaming, and running on the spot to get my feet up off the ground.

"Rats," Clodia screamed.

Then they started biting.

It was almost morning before the ship's company was able to get the plague of rats under control. Sailors equipped with broomsticks beat at them to disperse them from the main pack, ten thousand strong, and then stamped on the stragglers with their heavy-soled boots. A recorded message blasted from the public address system throughout the night, saying in a robotic voice:

"Third-class passengers remain calm, do not panic."

But despite the instruction, the passengers continued their frenzied rampage. When finally the last of the rats had been thwacked out of our cabin by a sailor with a pointed face, beady eyes, and twitching whiskers, I collapsed into my bunk exhausted. Clodia hoisted herself up the ladder and squeezed in beside me. I didn't have the strength to repel her.

"Freda, will you be my special friend?" she asked me tenderly.

This time I didn't need to pretend to be asleep. I really was dead to the world. I had a horrible dream about being on the cruise ship from hell, but when I woke up I knew I hadn't been dreaming.

sixteen

The day following the plague of rats was a full day at sea, which was just as well, because I needed to rest before our expedition to the pyramids the day after. The third-class deck was strewn with squashed rat parts: fur, tails, guts, ears, and teeth, and smears of blood covered the walls and floors.

Many people, including Clodia, had been bitten, and the ship's doctor became so overworked that a hastily written sign went up outside the sick bay, informing all passengers that from then on the medical service was available *only* to those in first and second class.

Dark rumblings were heard about a revolt, and groups of insurgents huddled conspiratorially in corners, but soon enough the ringleaders were led away on the express orders of the captain, and were never seen again.

I dressed Clodia's wounds as best I could, with the same skill and care with which I prepared corpses for funerals, and, worryingly, she swore her everlasting devotion to me. Gently, but firmly, I told her I liked boys, and that twice I had even held a willy in my hand. Yet it seemed to make no difference to her. The light of love burned undiminished in her eyes, and she followed me around everywhere like a puppy.

Another person who seemed to be everywhere was the short, fat man who had disturbed me in the deck chair the day before. Always accompanied by the black cardboard suitcase, he monopolized the third-class paddling pool (typically, the swimming pool and Jacuzzi were reserved for first and second class). He managed to get the only sun lounger that wasn't broken, the only table tennis bat (although it wasn't of much use to him), and at lunchtime he was seen devouring a round of ham sandwiches when everybody knew ham was restricted to first-class consumption. He had friends in high places, everybody had to agree.

Yet, during the afternoon, it began to occur to me that the short, fat man was following me. If I stood at the rail looking out to sea, insidiously he would appear at my side with his suitcase, clamping his hairpiece to his head (already I had witnessed three being lost overboard). If I took a stroll, he would be at my elbow, dragging the case behind him. If I rested momentarily on a bench, he would sit so close I could feel the heat of his body through his sailor suit, and sense the rhythmic undulation of his flesh with each breath.

To make matters worse, Clodia had scented a rival and glued herself to my other side. It felt like a three-legged race, and I was the leg in the middle. It was claustrophobic and hot in the depths of the huddle, and they defied all my efforts to shake them off. I fantasized about pushing them both into the sea. I grew resentful and angry. I just wanted to be alone.

I cast around for the other inmates of the short, fat man's institution. There were a good many candidates, but as they were in plain clothes instead of their uniforms, it was hard to know for sure. I resolved to find the matron and point out that he was bothering me. Maybe they could increase his doses of medication, or at least confine him to his cabin by strapping him into his bunk. But again this proved difficult; the nursing staff weren't in uniform either.

I was growing scratchy and disillusioned. I had managed only two hours sleep last night and that was in spite of Clodia. To think some people would give their right arm to go on a cruise. To me it was like a prison. I began to count the hours until I could go home. Twenty-four down; ninety-six to go. As each hour dragged itself past, mentally I checked it off. This was my focus, and my single consolation.

That night for dinner in the third-class dining room, we were served meat for the first time, which caused a brief feeling of euphoria among the carnivores. It wasn't a taste or a texture that I was familiar with, but there was plenty of it to go around; some people even had a second helping.

As we ate, rumors circulated around the long tables that there was to be a cabaret that evening in the Entertainment Room. None of us, of course, would be admitted, but it gave us a perverse sense of satisfaction to know what we were missing.

When she heard the news, Clodia, who was sitting so close to me that she was practically on my lap, became more than usually excited. Her eyes burned with a new fire, and her nose throbbed.

"Freda," she said dramatically, not caring who heard her, "I'm taking you to the cabaret!"

"How?" I replied. "We're not allowed in, and besides, you would be arrested the second you stepped a foot in first class."

I listened to what I had just said, and a bell pinged in my brain. If she was arrested, I would be free of her at last.

She thought for a while, during which time there was the

sound of distant tinkling, like a windup musical box, and then she said:

"I know, I'll go in disguise so they won't recognize me up there."

"Good idea!" I lied enthusiastically. Bingo!

Back in our cabin she struggled into one of the minidresses Fiamma had made me buy, and put on a pair of dark glasses.

"Would you know it was me, Freda?"

"Not in a million years."

Holding her mechanical hand (I thought I could allow her this final indulgence), we ran up the stairs. I was pleased to see that nearly all the rat corpses had by now been disposed of, and were no longer littering the gangways, causing people to skid on them and break their legs.

When we arrived panting at the first-class deck, I told Clodia that for the sake of safety, we had to separate until we got inside the Entertainment Room.

"They know we go everywhere together," I said. "They won't recognize you if you're alone."

Clodia looked at me with suspicion, as though sensing a trick.

"Then can we cuddle up together in the back row?" she asked.

I nodded, and stepped out into the vestibule, where I quickly mingled in with the crowd. I liked to think that even if I didn't look quite like a first-class person, I could easily pass for second-class. I took a glass of champagne from the tray of a passing waiter, ready to toast my freedom, and struck up a conversation with a gap-toothed woman wearing a mink stole and a tiara.

All the while I scanned the vestibule for signs of a rumpus that would indicate Clodia had been apprehended. Then, when the sound of a gong announced the cabaret was about to start, Clodia burst out of the stairwell like a cuckoo from a clock. The whole room went silent. It was clear to all there was an interloper in our midst. Immediately uniformed guards surrounded her.

"I'm not Clodia Strozzi," she stammered. "I'm someone else. You have to believe me."

It was no use. In a well-drilled motion the guards shuffled her back into the stairwell. Before the door clanged shut, I caught her eye for a moment, and I could see clearly in it the pain of love, longing, and despair.

seventeen

I swallowed my champagne too quickly, hurried into the Entertainment Room, and fell into the first empty seat I saw, hoping nobody had noticed me. I felt guilty about what had happened to Clodia, and nervous because I knew I was breaking the rules. Suppose I too was arrested?

Yet, at the same time, I was exhilarated. I wasn't used to champagne (in fact I had never had it before), and I think it had gone to my head. Something about the Entertainment Room—the dim lighting, low-pitched murmurs, a sense of expectation, the odors mingling in the air (French perfume, cigar smoke, cognac, a certain brand of furniture polish)—reminded me of the cabaret clubs where Mamma used to perform.

When she was younger, before Fiamma and I were born, Mamma had sung on cruise liners, and had traveled all over the world. I fantasized that she had met our father on a ship, although he was a total mystery, a forbidden subject that was never discussed. Perhaps it was in a room just like this one.

I could imagine him, like a character from a silent film, handsome and sophisticated, mustachioed probably, in a dinner jacket and bow tie, carnation in his lapel, sitting alone at one of the little tables, a glass of whiskey in his hand in which the ice cubes clinked. Perhaps, between his slightly yellow teeth a fat cigar glowed, its aroma combining in a cloud with his expensive eau de cologne.

Up on the stage, the curtains drew back revealing Mamma in a spotlight and a slinky black dress. Her hair was piled high; her smile was dazzling.

When their eyes met, time froze, the audience, the cocktail waitresses, and the band, all melted into nothingness, the tinkling of the piano died gracefully away, and immediately it was love, except, of course it wasn't Mamma, it was the Great Fango, the magician.

I roused from my reverie to see him produce the usual rabbits from a top hat, hard-boiled eggs from the mouths of the ladies in the audience, and doves from the ear canals of the gentlemen.

There followed fire-eaters, jugglers, two comedians, and a troupe of acrobats who performed amazing feats with a bottle, an orange, and a piece of string. After the interval, dancing girls in the skimpiest of costumes gyrated around to the numbers performed by Mel Cartouche, the international artiste: "There's a Kind of Hush," "Michelle," and "I'll Never Fall in Love Again." Admittedly his strong Polish accent made them sound somewhat strange, compared to the original versions, but he endowed them with his own charm, and I have to say, he had a very powerful voice. In fact, listening to him made me long to sing too, and although I wouldn't claim to have a voice like Mamma's, I prided myself that I had inherited a little of her talent.

All too soon, the final act was announced, and the shock of it left me reeling, feeling dizzy and weak. The last act was a ventriloquist. Yes. A ventriloquist! The unparalleled, the extraordinary, Alberto Lippi. My brain was flooded with the recollection of Mamma's dying prophesy, "Fredina . . . I see a ventriloquist . . ." Yet until now, I had never come across one.

When the curtains opened again, I sat up straight and craned my neck to see between the woman at the table in front of mine with the enormous shrub of hair (honestly, it was so big that some of the magician's doves had built a nest in it) and her companion, who had the ears of an elephant.

To my absolute and overwhelming astonishment, framed between them both, I beheld the short, fat man I had first encountered in the deck chair, up on the stage, with a dummy of almost equal size seated primly on his knee. My heart sank until it came to rest in my stomach. So he was the ventriloquist. My first thought was that I could never, ever, have sex with him.

He introduced the dummy as Malco the naughty schoolboy.

"I'm not naughty," squeaked the dummy.

"I'm afraid he is naughty, ladies and gentlemen," the ventriloquist replied. "Only the other day . . ."

The two went through their predictable routine, but I have to say that when the dummy was talking, the voice did actually seem to come out of him, and certainly the mouth of the small, fat man never moved a muscle.

At the end of this part of the act, the small, fat man told the schoolboy it was his bedtime, and had to coax him into his case. The big black suitcase I recognized. Even when the dummy was shut away, he continued muttering and his voice was muffled by the lid of the case, and finally his complaints were replaced by gentle snores and whimpers.

Then the ventriloquist began to throw his voice among the audience. He put his words into the mouth of a burly, beefy man and made him sound like a eunuch. He gave a countess the voice and vocabulary of a vulgar fishwife. A young girl was made to sing like Frank Sinatra, and all the time, on the stage, the short, fat man stood in silence, seemingly saying nothing.

Then, as the finale was about to begin, the captain's voice came over the public address system, calling for us to abandon ship. Just as the panic set in and the ladies started screaming and were hoisting up their evening dresses preparing to run for their lives, a plant in the audience started the thunderous applause. It had been the ventriloquist, of course, having the last laugh.

The passengers filed out of the Entertainment Room, laughing and chattering, and I looked around nervously for the guards before making my escape. As I reached the door, I heard a voice, a man's voice, whispering inside my ear, so close it tickled. It said my name over and over again:

"Freda, Freda, Freda."

I looked rapidly around me. There was nobody there. I shivered, and felt a prickling sensation at the base of my skull. As I walked away the voice said softly:

"I am your destiny."

I scuttled downstairs like a beetle. It was after the curfew and the third-class deck was blacker than the night. I felt my way back to what I hoped was the right cabin. Inside I fumbled beneath my mattress for the candle and matches I had managed to acquire earlier that day on the black market that was already flourishing in third class. In the flickering light, for which I had traded a bathing costume and a bread roll (buttered), I was amazed at what I saw.

Every trace of Clodia had been erased. All the shirtwaist dresses I had swapped with her were gone. This was a bitter blow. Now I would have to wear my own unsuitable clothes. The very whiff of her had vanished, as had her plush panda pajama case, and her gray and repellent underwear, which she'd festooned like bunting around her bunk. Her toothbrush and candy-flavored toothpaste were missing. Even the giant petrol can had gone. It really was as though Clodia Strozzi had never existed.

Perhaps, though, and this thought cheered me, the authorities had simply removed her stuff and taken it for her convenience to her place of detention. Yes, that was it. It was good that she had those familiar things around her.

I climbed into my bunk, congratulating myself on the fact that I had had the foresight to use the first-class powder room while I was upstairs. The third-class washroom hadn't been decontaminated since the start of the cruise, if indeed then, and besides the ever-present queue made access near impossible.

I snuffed out the candle, not wishing to waste it, and lay back thinking of the ventriloquist. I couldn't get him out of my mind. I could still hear that voice whispering in my ear. I could feel the tickle of breath that formed those words:

"Freda . . . I am your destiny."

Was it really true?

As I dozed I remember hearing an enormous splash coupled with the sort of gulp that a body of deep water makes when it swallows something heavy. Then I slept a thick, dreamless sleep.

eighteen

At five AM the Klaxon sounded in third class.

"All rise. All rise," insisted the robotic voice.

There was an air of happy excitement as we scrambled to get ready. We were coming into harbor at Port Said, for our once-in-a-lifetime visit to the Sphinx and the pyramids. I still remember the thrill of standing on the deck in the fresh new air, watching the shore draw near, seeing all the boats and bustling action of the port, and behind it the domes and minarets, the huge advertising billboards, jostling blocks of flats, and plenteous palm trees that herald the traveler's arrival in that fascinating maritime city. For those moments of joy, it had all been worthwhile; I wouldn't have missed it for anything.

There was the usual delay as we moored, and then, class by class, like in school, we were allowed to disembark onto the pontoon of floating oilcans that led to the dockside. I loved the pontoon. The bobbing up and down. I thought of Clodia. I know she would have liked it too.

Once through customs we emerged into Egypt, and a heat that was like a bread oven. Immediately my senses came alive. My eyes smarted at the incredible intensity of the light, and colors seemed so bright: blinding blues, reds, yellows, the whitest possible whites. The air was filled with an exciting din: the call to prayer from the minarets filled me with delight; the cries of the street vendors were wonderfully exotic; even the roar of traffic and sirens seemed new and mysterious. Smells bombarded my nostrils: diesel fumes, drains, cumin, overripe bananas, roasting goat flesh, melting tarmac, garbage, dung.

I was in love with the place already.

The stewards directed us to the dusty parking area in front of the customs shed, where first- and second-class passengers embarked on their air-conditioned luxury coaches that boasted a chemical lavatory and hostess service providing ice-cold drinks and gastronomic nibbles.

We in third class were to take local transport. So much

the better, I thought. I would much rather experience the real Egypt than be in a hermetically sealed pod.

While we waited for our bus, the luxury coaches pulled away. Some of the occupants waved. None of us waved back. The sun grew hotter by the minute. Soon we were beset by a gang of small children offering cool water from a glass tank with half a lemon floating in it. The lemon didn't appear to be in the first flush of youth, but no doubt it was flavorsome. Other children offered postcards of camels wearing sun hats, fezzes made of felt, packets of biscuits, toffee apples, chewing gum, and slices of mango. They were cheeky little fellows, and reluctant to take no for an answer. When their sales techniques were becoming threatening rather than endearing, a police officer approached and beat them away with a stick.

By this time the more anxious of the sightseers began consulting their wristwatches with increasing urgency, and demanded to know when our bus would be coming. But I was enjoying myself; it was part of the adventure, after all.

Finally, after a delay of about two and a half hours, during which three of our number developed sunstroke and had to be taken back to the ship, a bus drew into the parking area, sending clouds of rich red dust up into the air. Even the dust was more appealing than our own Roman dust. At first the driver kept the doors firmly shut and wouldn't let us in, even though some of the gentlemen in our group threatened him through the window with their fists. Then, when at last he did open the doors, out of nowhere came a swarm of local people who surged onto the bus accompanied by their herds of animals and children. The cruisers fought back and pushed their way in, although the maximum capacity was soon exceeded and many of the third-class passengers were forced to stand for the entire five-hour journey.

I was fortunate to get a window seat next to a jolly big lady swathed in black robes who carried a cabbage of monstrous size on her head. Behind were her five little children and a sheep, which seemed overcome by the heat. Beyond them, I was amazed to see the ventriloquist. How had he managed to get on board without my seeing him? He was cooling himself with a fan of flamingo feathers, and above his head—in the luggage rack stuffed with chickens, watermelons, sugar cane, and kettles—was the big black suitcase.

I was delighted with my view from the window and kept my eyes glued to the constantly changing kaleidoscope of interest. Yet I could not feel entirely comfortable with the ventriloquist so near.

The bus baked, and the occupants gave off a riper odor, and the noxious fumes of the traffic penetrated the open window and mixed with the vapors created by some of the passengers who had lit fires to boil up stews or roast slabs of mutton. The bleating of the sheep and lambs, the gobbling of the geese, the lilting conversation in Arabic of my fellow travelers—everything had the mesmerizing, confusing quality of a dream. And as I succumbed to the heat and the fug, I imagined other voices that seemed to come from far, far away:

"Why her?"

"You know why: because Madame Jo-Jo never gets it wrong."

"Puh! You and your fortune-tellers! What do they know? And what about me?"

"It won't change a thing between us, trust me. You know we'll be together forever."

I slept. It had been such an early start, and I had been sleep deprived since I left home. I woke up some hours later to find the bus had broken down, far from the port, but way before reaching the pyramids. We were marooned. The driver was brewing hibiscus tea at the side of the road. A man had tethered his buffalo in the shade, and was milking it into a pail. My neighbor handed me a slice of succulent watermelon, with a completely toothless smile. I took it gratefully. She sucked a slice herself with relish and spat the seeds out with a splat. Around me the ship's passengers had collapsed like flies, groaning. Chickens pecked among their sprawling forms. The ventriloquist was still in his seat two rows behind. Beads of sweat stood out on his brow and on his upper lip. In the luggage rack Malco was strangely silent.

We never did get to see the pyramids or the Sphinx. The bus remained at the roadside for the rest of the day, and into the night. At sunset we were passed by the luxury coaches containing the first and second classes, on the opposite side of the highway, returning to the port. Sometime later another local bus was sent out to retrieve us and we were driven back at frightening speed to reach the cruise ship before it sailed. The ventriloquist was glued to my side during the return journey. Neither of us spoke.

As we bobbed across the pontoon, just as the *Santa Domenica* was about to weigh anchor, I turned to the short, fat man and said:

"I'm agreeing to nothing until I've consulted my parrot." And then I left him without a backward glance.

nineteen

The climax of the cruise was now over, and the ship was heading back to Civitavecchia. We were on the home run, and there was an air of anticipation that affected the first- and second-class passengers and the crew. In third class, it was very different. An air of failure, of melancholy, hung over the lowest deck like a cloud. The whole purpose of the trip had been denied us, and there was talk of a conspiracy among the more suspicious-minded. People became depressed; their spirits were crushed.

And what made matters worse was when Rula Argenti developed dysentery, and in the unsanitary conditions belowdecks, it spread like a forest fire. The resigned queue that waited without hope outside the single lavatory that soon became horribly blocked discussed the cause of the epidemic:

"It was that lemon-flavored water we drank in the parking lot," said Fantasia Spiga, struggling to control the eruption she could feel brewing within her.

"No, it was the chicken stew they cooked up on the bus," said Nero Pupa. "We never should have tried it."

"It was the buffalo milk," countered Nicoletta Bellini. "That evil-looking creature was responsible for it all."

So far, I had avoided the contagion, and tried to spend most of the day on the sundeck, where I hoped the sea breezes would keep the germs at bay.

At my side, constantly, was the ventriloquist, for the first time without the suitcase. The dummy was, apparently, suffering from heat exhaustion after the day spent in the luggage rack of the bus, and was having to lie down in their cabin with a damp washcloth on his head.

I'm not quite sure how it happened, but already we had assumed the diaphanous mantle of a couple. Unintentionally we walked in step along the decks. Instinctively we moved in unison toward an empty bench for a rest, an enticing patch of shade, or an interesting sight out at sea. The ventriloquist drew rogue strands of hair out of my eyes. I plucked fluff from the collar of his sailor suit, or snatched for his hairpiece when it took flight.

When we encountered the captain near the bridge, the

ventriloquist introduced me as Freda Castro, his fiancée. I wasn't surprised.

Neither of us felt the need to say very much. We had the practiced ease of people who have been together for a long, long time. Who know the other's stories, and smile generously at their well-worn anecdotes. Who can anticipate what the other will say before they open their lips. And who can feel their presence without looking by virtue of their scent in the air, the sound of their footsteps, and the invisible strings that bind us together. Yet in this we were mistaken, for we were absolute strangers to each other.

Looking back on it, I certainly wasn't attracted to the ventriloquist. Alberto, as I shall call him now. But I didn't really know what attraction was. I hadn't felt it before. I certainly had felt no attraction to Ernesto Porcino, just curiosity about his body. Yet, like Alberto, I was convinced of the inevitability of it all. I put my faith in Mamma. She saw my future with a ventriloquist. In all probability, it was this one.

The final night at sea there was to be a gala. The captain's original intention had been to include even the third-class passengers to compensate them in some small way for missing the cruise's highlight. He was considering ways of limiting them to soft drinks, because he didn't want them getting tipsy, and was creating a two-tiered system with respect to other refreshments, but the calculations and diagrams he produced on a sheaf of papers proved unnecessary.

When the attack of dysentery worsened, he knew the lower deck couldn't be involved in the festivities for fear of contaminating the superior classes. Soon he was forced to put the whole of third class into quarantine.

I returned to my deck to find it sealed off with tape, and notices saying "Infected area. Danger of death. Do not enter." From inside the controlled zone came the sound of distant weeping.

And so it came about that I moved into Alberto's cabin, although nothing of an intimate nature took place between us, I can assure you. He was in the entertainers' area, on the personnel deck, sandwiched between second class and the engine rooms. The dummy was obliged to relinquish his bunk to me and return to his suitcase, and although he complained, Alberto stood firm. The dummy took against me after that, and although I tried to be friendly toward him, he never forgave me.

I managed to borrow an outfit from one of the dancing girls, and the gala evening was the best night of my life. Alberto was magnificent. His act was even better than before, and I felt proud of him. Yes, proud. The other ladies in the audience looked at me with expressions of understanding, approval, and possibly even envy in one or two cases, and I blushed and was coy. The voice in my ear whispered:

"Marry me, Freda,"

and I whispered back:

"It depends on my parrot."

Dancing followed the cabaret. It was held on the first-class sundeck, where an area had been specially prepared with a portable polished surface. Alberto was a wonderful dancer. So light on his feet—not like a fat man at all. And although he only came up to my shoulder, I think we made a handsome couple. We whirled around the dance floor at dizzying speed, and Alberto knew all the steps: the samba, the mambo, the jive. We even performed the tango, which drew us a round of applause from the onlookers.

We were still dancing when the Klaxon sounded and the captain gave the order to abandon ship. This time, it wasn't Alberto playing a trick.

We never found out what really happened. It was a calm and romantic night, lit by a canopy of twinkling stars paying homage to the new moon. The sea was gently undulating like ruffled silk. There was hardly a breath of wind.

A torpedo fired by a Russian submarine was one of the more imaginative theories put forward. Negligence. Metal fatigue. Act of God. Act of the Devil. All were considered by the investigating authorities. More likely, however, was an act of sabotage by one or more of the third-class passengers. Some, I knew, were dangerously close to the edge. Some were simply unable to take any more.

Whatever the explanation, the ship quickly began to sink. Unlike in the shipwrecks you see in the movies, there was no panic—no hysterical ladies, or gentlemen firing revolvers and disguising themselves as grandmothers to get a place in the lifeboats. The members of the band didn't continue playing: they put down their instruments and marshaled at their station. The captain didn't remain stoically on the bridge.

The lifeboats were lowered in orderly fashion, and there were more than enough of them too, at least for the first- and second-class passengers, the entertainment corps, and the crew.

Belowdecks, the third-class passengers who had survived the dysentery had already drowned. Only the upper deck was still above the level of the sea. Alberto stripped off his dinner jacket and was about to dive down one of the internal staircases to rescue Malco, but before he could do so, there was a bubbling under the water and the schoolboy appeared wearing a pair of small red swimming trunks and a scuba diver's mask. He gave Alberto an arch look, strode over to a lifeboat in which he took his place, and wrapped himself up in a blanket. As the waves lapped around the hem of my borrowed gown, we knew it was time for us, too, to leave. We stepped into the lifeboat, the sailors rowed us swiftly away, and with a gentle motion the *Santa Domenica* slipped silently beneath the waves.

The lifeboats bobbed together like floating corks. The only sounds were the gentle plash of the ripples against the sides of the boats, and the subdued whispers of the survivors.

It seemed like no time before the minesweeper HMS *Clover* rescued us, and by midmorning we were steaming into Civitavecchia. How relieved I felt to see my home port coming closer and closer into view. While we were still some way out, I heard the notes of a brass band wafting from the quay. Bunting had been strung up, and there were some slightly deflated balloons.

Soon I was able to see my own little welcoming party on the quayside, and tears filled my eyes. The little group was just the same, standing in the same places as they had been to see me off. Was that really only five days ago? What a lot of life I had lived since then.

At a little distance I could make out Clodia's mother, waving her mechanical hand at another woman she had mistaken for her daughter, crying with relief under the false impression she had survived.

Finally, finally, I disembarked into the waiting arms of my loved ones, with Alberto standing shyly at my side, and Malco shuffling his feet impatiently in the dust. Pierino perched immediately on my shoulder and stroked his beak along my cheek, first one side, then the other, with the motion you would use to sharpen a knife.

Signora Dorotea was the first to clasp me to her bosom, which snubbed Aunt Ninfa, who thought hers should be the prior claim. Signora Dorotea's voice was almost incomprehensible through her tears.

"My poor girl," she cried, "to think all this was my idea. You could have died out there, and it would have been my fault."

"Yes, you should be ashamed of yourself," chipped in Aunt Ninfa, seizing her angle and her opportunity, "putting ideas in her head. Foreign travel indeed! Egypt! Why, what's natural is to live and die within the sound of your own bells. Leave what's foreign to the foreigners, that's what I say."

Just as things threatened to turn nasty between the two women, the photographer from *Mortician's Monthly* rushed over. The shipwreck was an unexpected bonus to the editorial department at the magazine. They hadn't had a single idea for the July issue before this; now they could stretch it out to fill a double-page spread with full-color advertisement inserts.

Aunt Ninfa rounded on the photographer. She wasn't usually aggressive, but it was the result of stress: she had been worried sick until the authorities had been able to confirm my name was on the survivors list.

"Sensationalist reporting, that's all it is," she said, beating him with her cheap paper fan. "These dreadful paparazzi."

All was grist for the photographer's mill, and he continued clicking his shutter.

Clodia's mother was wandering from welcome party to welcome party calling for her daughter to appear, but of course everybody knew poor Clodia wasn't coming back.

"Is he bothering you?" asked Polibio, jerking his head toward Alberto. The two had been sizing each other up in an uneasy silence, and each was ready for combat.

"He's the ventriloquist," I said, by way of an answer.

"We're engaged," he said, causing a stunned reaction that seemed to suspend all activity in the dockyard. The cranes stopped loading containers onto ships; seagulls ceased flying and hung motionless in the air; the brass band paused, and their booming notes died away. Horns fell silent. Sailors, stevedores, and strumpets stood still.

The only motion was a flurry of feathers that rumpled the still air, and Pierino landed on the tip of Alberto's nose. Momentarily they looked deep into each other's eyes, and it was love. Pierino displayed his whole armory of affection. He nibbled Alberto's ears delicately. He laid his head endearingly upon his shoulder. He performed somersaults around his outstretched finger. He stood on the hairpiece and flapped his wings, all the while cooing with a baby voice; the parrots' mating call.

"I love you," said Pierino passionately, the first words he had ever spoken.

"You see, he loves me," Alberto whispered.

I knew then that I would marry him, and my heart sank.

twenty

Alberto had not, it transpired, made a favorable impression on my friends and relatives.

"You can't marry him," said Signora Dorotea when I returned to work the next day.

"I don't know what it is about him," she continued, in her agitation piling too many cotton flocks into the cheeks of Signor Stufo, so that he began to resemble a hamster. "Yes," she said, pulling them all out and starting over again, "I don't know what it is about him, but it isn't right."

This feeling was echoed by Uncle Birillo and Aunt Ninfa, who insisted I join them for dinner.

"I know you've just had the most terrible experience," began Uncle Birillo over artichokes braised with spearmint and lots of garlic, "and of course, it hasn't been easy for you since you lost your dear mamma, rest her soul." Here he exchanged worried glances with Aunt Ninfa to check if he was doing all right. He was.

"And your aunt and I care very deeply about you; you know that."

I nodded. I knew where all this was leading. Then Aunt Ninfa burst out. She couldn't help herself, cutting straight through Uncle Birillo's carefully constructed beginning.

"Don't do it, Freda," she shrieked. "Don't marry that horrible little man. It will end in disaster; I know it will. Raffaello says . . ."

"For the love of the Madonna," interrupted Uncle Birillo, banging the table with his fists in exasperation. "Can't you for once in your life keep your mouth shut?"

Whereupon Aunt Ninfa broke into great racking sobs that made the neighbors rush in, fearing the worst.

"As I was trying to say, Freda," he resumed after shepherding the residents back onto the landing, "it's only natural, given the trauma you have suffered in your life, that you should long for happiness, stability, the comfort of the special relationship between a man and a woman, but marriage isn't a step to be taken lightly, believe me. I'm not saying this ventriloquist fellow isn't right for you . . ."

"Of course he isn't right for her," screamed Aunt Ninfa. "What are you saying, Birillo?"

Ignoring her, Uncle Birillo continued,

"But you've only known him a few days, and under the most dreadful circumstances. Think it over carefully; that's all I'm asking you to do. Don't rush into anything, promise me?"

"Promise," I lied.

As I left I heard Aunt Ninfa raging inside the building. "Birillo, that man is sinister, I tell you. He's playing some kind of game with her; you mark my words . . ."

That night, or rather in the early hours of the next morning, I received a mysterious phone call. First someone was talking in Spanish, and I assumed I had got a crossed line. Then there was a degree of graininess and crackling. Then there came a voice I recognized. It was Fiamma. She was calling from Paraguay, where she was holding secret talks with the government. Concerned about the news she had received by telex, Fiamma had interrupted the talks at a crucial stage to come to the phone.

There were several times when I could hear nothing, but

Fiamma carried on talking; so our conversation was confused, but I got the general gist of what she was saying.

"Freda, you're making a massive mistake," she said at the end.

"You did the same," I replied.

"That's different," she snapped, and the line went dead.

twenty-one

The following morning the headlines of *La Repubblica* made me choke on my coffee:

CRUISE HORROR:

THE NIGHTMARE CONTINUES

The article went on:

A fishing trawler, the *Santa Isolda,* made an unusual discovery when it hoisted its nets in the Golfo di Noto at noon yesterday. Along with the sea bream, gilthead, sardines, and assorted crustaceans, the net bulged with what was at first considered a rare Melon-headed whale

(*Peponocephala*). However, on closer examination it was found to have a thick head of hair encrusted with barnacles and baby crabs. The superstitious sailors from Pozzallo (Ragusa Province) believed they had fished up a mermaid and were divided in their opinions as to whether this augured well or ill, when the creature in the net astounded them all by beginning to speak. Although incoherent, the creature, which was later identified as a woman, kept repeating the name of the luxury cruise liner, the *Santa Domenica,* that had sunk in the Malta Channel the previous night under suspicious circumstances. It seems this survivor had swum an astonishing seventy kilometers from the site of the sinking, before becoming enmeshed in the trawler's nets. Despite receiving the best of care from the ship's crew, the woman died before reaching hospital at Avola. Her last words were, cryptically, "Tell Freda I love her." The woman, naked, and weighing 100 kilos, had an unusual mechanical left hand that had suffered corrosion from contact with the seawater. She carried no formal identification but was later named through dental records as one Clodia Strozzi of the San Basilio district of Roma. The cause of death was given by the coroner as exhaustion, exposure, and saltwater inhala-

tion. She is survived by her mother, also Clodia. The Perfect Luxury shipping line that owned the fated vessel expressed its deepest sympathies to Signora Strozzi last night. "Signora Strozzi (junior) was the life and soul of the party on our recent phenomenally successful 'Magic of the Pharoes' Cruise. Her fellow passengers will remember fondly her exuberant dancing, her sparkling wit, and her huge capacity for fun. Sadly, her like will not be seen again," said a spokesman.

So Clodia had survived after all, only to perish. And to think that her last words had been for me. I felt terrible.

It was not long before a reporter from the scurrilous rag *Dirty Gossip* was sniffing round the reception desk of the funeral parlor asking probing questions.

"Could you comment on the nature of the relationship between Freda Castro, your embalmer, and the deceased woman?" he asked insinuatingly of Signora Dorotea while I hid in the chapel of rest.

"No, I could not," Signora Dorotea replied, driving him out with the threat of a hypodermic needle in the groin.

As I set off at lunchtime to be introduced to Alberto's family, I wore dark glasses, just in case the paparazzi were lurking outside.

Signora Dorotea couldn't resist a final word.

"I tell you, Freda, you're making a big mistake. It's a holiday romance; that's all it is. We've all had them, even me. I was young myself once, you know. His name was Siro. In Canneto it was, one August. I was twelve at the time, or was it thirteen? Just like you thought, full of hormones, no sense. He had the biggest marble collection I've ever seen."

"I'll get you a meringue on my way back," I said, knowing how to divert her.

"Ooh, lovely," she said. "Yes, please."

I felt quite nervous when I was introduced to Signora Lippi, and to Alberto's sister, Nunziata, and her brood, which at that time numbered five.

The signora looked at me for a long time without speaking. Then she turned to Alberto and said simply:

"Son, don't marry her."

Then Nunziata chipped in and said to her brother:

"I don't like her."

Afterward Alberto said:

"I think it went rather well."

But I'm pretty certain he was lying.

twenty-two

Despite this opposition, we set the date, and at that time I think we were united by the predominant view that we were a disaster waiting to happen. At least we had this much in common.

On Saturday June 24, 1972, at five PM we were married.

My only satisfaction was knowing that I had fulfilled Mamma's prophecy.

The wedding ceremony, which took place in the Municipio in the Via Giulia, just a few blocks from our old apartment, was a joyless charade. In fact, I have been to funerals that were far more jolly. At the entrance, Polibio, who was wearing a false nose in an ill-advised attempt at humor, handed out paper handkerchiefs to dry the tears of the many guests who were crying. Aunt Ninfa was inconsolable, and her bellows were even louder than when we buried Mamma, and Signora Pucillo.

"I can't help it, Birillo," she howled, before my uncle could open his lips to berate her. "When I look at that nasty, ugly, slimy, creepy, little man, I just can't bear it."

"Don't upset yourself, Ninfa," said Fiamma, trying to be cheerful. "It won't last, so why worry?" But soon even the Secret Service operatives that surrounded her were sobbing.

The formalities were concluded at a rapid pace, which left me in a blur. I said "Yes" to every question asked of me, without reflecting. I willed my nerve to hold, and focused on externals: the wooden sound of Malco's teeth gnashing in the row immediately behind; the grunting breathing of Nunziata's brood, dressed uniformly in black knickerbockers and caps; the gibbering of Signora Lippi; and the overwhelming stagnant odor of the bridegroom by my side.

The only happy one was Pierino. He stood on Signora Dorotea's shoulder, flapping his wings, and barking in imitation of a dog, which signaled his true and deep delight.

Afterward, there was no reception, no cake, no dancing, no gifts, or confetti. What would be the point? To celebrate would have been hypocritical.

So Alberto hired a pony and trap to drive us to the station

from where we would take the train to Fregene to spend our wedding night at the celebrated hotel the Villa Spugnea.

The guests on my side went back to Aunt Ninfa's to swap dire predictions about our married life (some of which proved remarkably accurate), and at the same time to drown their sorrows in Uncle Birillo's homemade coffee liqueur.

What Alberto's family did, I couldn't say.

twenty-three

I would prefer to draw a veil over the technical details of our disastrous wedding night. Everything that could go wrong did. Although Alberto had reserved the honeymoon suite, the Villa Spugnea had no record of this, and claimed it was unavailable. In fact, although the hotel was deserted, the receptionist assured us that every room was occupied.

She did suggest the possibility of a broom cupboard, which, if we were prepared to wait long enough, she could have someone show us. We kicked our heels in the empty corridors for an hour, then two, and finally the housekeeper, who had been a Rumanian shot-putter in a previous existence, showed us with little enthusiasm up to the attic floor.

The broom cupboard proved to be a typical broom cupboard, equipped with a variety of mops, brushes, antiquated sweepers, and dented pails. It was thick with dust, which was responsible for starting an attack of the quick-fire sneezing to which Alberto had been subject ever since he was a boy. The shot-putter informed us that for an additional twenty thousand lire on top of the room rate, a camp bed could be erected. Enthusiastically—too enthusiastically, I felt—Alberto agreed.

We waited for this service, and for our luggage to be delivered, and all the while Alberto sneezed with the deafening rapidity of a machine gun.

I wish I could say that during this time my bridegroom and I seethed with a passion for one other's flesh, but we didn't. Instead Alberto sneezed, and I balanced on an upturned bucket, trying to suppress the question that kept forcing itself into my mind: "What am I doing here?" This situation reminded me of that time on the gangplank of the cruise liner, when I had resisted the impulse to run away, and I had been wrong. Should I escape this time, before it was too late?

At that critical moment the shot-putter arrived with our luggage and the camp bed, which she assembled with much muttering and an excess of bad grace. We had to pay her an awful lot of money to go away. Each attempt at satisfying her with a tip failed, and she continued to hold her hand outstretched, with a menacing look in her eye.

At last we were alone. Well, almost alone. Although Alberto had promised to leave Malco behind at his mother's, for relations between the puppet and me had deteriorated since our return from the cruise, I had reason to suspect Alberto had smuggled the schoolboy along. True, he had abandoned the replacement black suitcase in which the dummy regularly traveled, but instead there was a red one of similar size and weight, and whose contents he refused to reveal, and wouldn't explain.

"Just a harmless little secret, my love," he had murmured before the attack of sneezing rendered him red, wet, and dumb. But already his relationship with the dummy was causing the gentle ringing of an alarm bell in a corner of my brain.

We stood awkwardly in the now crowded broom cupboard, waiting for what would happen next—for love, I suppose, but it didn't happen.

Alberto couldn't stop sneezing. It was pointless to try, so he held his nostrils closed with the finger and thumb of one hand and started removing his clothes with the other. I tried to help. It was the least I could do under the circumstances.

We got him out of his jacket, shoes, and pants, his shirt and tie, but stopped at his undershirt and shorts and his socks. It seemed too blatant really, to continue further. I tried not to notice his gray flesh—the color of an unembalmed corpse, and the aroma of wet dog that hung about him.

With a sinking heart, I realized it was now my turn. Reluctantly I removed my funeral suit and blouse with the same embarrassment you have in stripping prior to medical examination.

There was then the problem of what to do with the clothes, which now occupied the camp bed. Together we worked to hang them from the handles of the brooms and mops to keep them out of the dust. We took our time over this task. There was no need to rush. We adjusted things until we were pleased with the results, and felt the satisfaction of a job well done.

I would really have liked to go home then.

At last we knew we had to approach the camp bed. There could be no more prevarication. Taking the lead, Alberto eased himself into it in a way that took me straight back to that deck chair on the *Santa Domenica,* when I had seen him for the first time, and was revolted by him. The springs groaned, and considered giving up. One did, and there was a lurch as the canvas ripped, causing Alberto to bang his head on the floor. Doubtless we would be required to pay for the damage.

With his free hand, he beckoned me to join him. Quite clearly there wasn't the room, or the strength in the frame, but I lowered myself gingerly until I was on top of him. Then the remaining springs buckled, and the canvas separated from the frame with the motion of a snake shedding its skin. We were now on the floor, with the frame looking down on us from above like a viewing gallery. The sound of sniggering came from the red suitcase.

So much for the preliminaries. It is not surprising that I failed to arouse Alberto's passion as conclusively as he failed to ignite mine. I don't honestly believe he had any more of an idea as to what to do than I did.

"Not like that, it won't work," he managed to sneeze as I tackled his tiny pink thing in the same way that I had manipulated Ernesto's purple one the previous summer. So I held his nose for him while he tried, but he was no more successful than I was. It was excruciating.

I remember with a shudder his hands that felt like slabs of hot lard smeared on my skin. His sweat-drenched body, heavy as a dead weight, crushing me, the airlessness of the cupboard exacerbating the foul odors he emitted. The streaming mucus that pored from his mouth and nose. And, much later, when the sneezing eventually slowed and finally stopped, the voices began with their obscene comments and suggestions.

The morning was an extremely long time in coming. When the first feeble rays of the sun penetrated the skylight of the broom cupboard, I realized the truth: I hated Alberto. It was June 25, 1972, and the first day of our married life.

Now and Again

Obstinacy, I suppose, kept me from ending the marriage—I wouldn't admit that I had been wrong, and everybody else had been right. Of course, secretly I accepted that I had been a fool for marrying solely on the strength of Mamma's dying words—I had learned the hard way that prophecies are a load of nonsense. In the first few months, all sorts of people—even total strangers, like the woman whose poodle bit my bad leg in the Piazza Navona—urged me to leave Alberto, but after that they stopped mentioning it.

Fortunately, from the start, and without any need for discussion, he and I resumed our separate lives. I continued to put all my energies into my work, and was building quite a reputation for myself. With the escalating violence of the city, there were always new and fascinating challenges for me, and, of course, a growing workload. Murders, like everything else, tend to follow fashions. At one time there was a craze for ears to be cut off, then noses, then lips. The only time Signora Dorotea and I were really stumped was when the notorious gangster Tusco Gozzini had his whole face hacked off in the most vicious vendetta we had ever encountered. Although we managed to rebuild the missing features, the resulting face didn't resemble the Tusco of the "Wanted" posters everybody knew. Nevertheless, the family were terribly grateful for our efforts, and his widow even said she preferred him without the broken nose and the cauliflower ear.

What little free time I had, I devoted to Pierino, although he had, I knew, transferred his affections to the ventriloquist.

Alberto and the dummy remained on the cruise-liner circuit and were often absent for months at a stretch. Occasionally I would receive picture postcards from Sydney, the fjords, Alaska, or Madagascar, and I felt a bright moment of joy knowing they were so far away. Yet Pierino would pine all the time they were gone. His feathers fell out by the handful, and he would ask constantly, "Where's Papa? Where's Papa?" until both Signor Tontini and I were ready to scream.

When they returned (causing Pierino to collapse in paroxysms of delight), reluctantly I allowed them to stay at my apartment, although I insisted Malco remain in the suitcase. They performed where they could, and in addition to regular appearances at the Berenice cabaret club, they took bookings for kiddies' parties, corporate entertainments, and the magic grotto at the Condelli department store.

Although I didn't like Alberto, I wasn't unhappy. After all, I had no idea what marriage should be like. The only one I had seen at close quarters was Uncle Birillo and Aunt Ninfa's, and they certainly didn't seem to like each other. Did Fiamma like Polibio? I don't know—we never discussed it.

Of course, I felt just as frustrated as I had before the wedding, and if anything the rashes, palpitations, and embarrassing surges increased. From time to time I encountered Ernesto Porcino at trade fairs, but he ignored me. Besides, I was wary of having an affair—I knew replacing one unsatisfactory man with another wasn't the answer. Once or twice I tried masturbation, but I was no good at it.

"Well, Freda, what you never had you never miss," Signora Dorotea announced one day, apropos of nothing.

I supposed she was right, and tried to suppress all thoughts of a passionate nature, but when I met the Detective, all my old symptoms returned with a vengeance, and new ones—most disturbing, the fantasies—were added.

two

I intended to spend the whole of Sunday searching for Pierino, but I received an urgent call from Signora Dorotea, which I couldn't ignore. All twenty-seven residents of the Crepuscolo nursing home had died of botulism from canned sardines, and the coroner had just released the bodies for burial. We would have to act fast to embalm them all, particularly in this heat, as our cold storage facilities were already stretched to the limit. I hurried to the Vicolo Sugarelli, keeping my eyes peeled for Pierino, but I saw only a crow and two seagulls.

As I worked alongside Signora Dorotea, she said:

"That Detective's a bit of a dish, isn't he?"

"The Detective?" I was flummoxed. "Has he been here?"

"Oh, yes," she replied. "I had to help him with his inquiries. Nice eyes, I thought. And so tall. I like a tall man. Porzio was tall when I met him, but of course, age shrinks us all. Anyway I was thinking to myself, Freda could do a lot worse than that Detective . . ."

"So what was he asking?"

"Oh, you know, this and that. Wanted to know about Alberto. Nasty little creep, I said. Never liked him. Smelled funny. I happened to mention that the best thing for you would be to find a nice new man, a tall one this time . . ."

"You didn't!"

"I certainly did. He was interested, Freda; he was definitely interested . . ."

Knowing how subtle Signora Dorotea's hints were, I would never be able to face the Detective again. But for now he was the least of my worries. We worked all day and late into the night, restoring the Crepuscolo's residents to their former glory. The very final one turned out to be Signor Felice, Signora Pucillo's paramour. At first neither of us recognized him, for the sardine poisoning had ravaged his mellow charms, reducing him to a puckered and suppurating shadow of his former self. But by the time we finished with him, he looked just like Rudolph Valentino in *The Son of the Sheik.* Up in heaven, Signora Pucillo would be putty in his hands.

I fell into bed exhausted in the early hours of Monday

morning and hoped to sleep a little later than usual, but at eight the phone rang insistently and I had to pick it up.

"Freda, he's cheating on me," screamed Aunt Ninfa in my ear.

"No!" I shouted back, over the roar of traffic noise in the background.

"How much longer are you going to be in there?" yelled someone else. "I need to call a doctor."

There was the sound of a scuffle, and then Aunt Ninfa came back on the line panting.

"He's been to confession," she bellowed. "That man hasn't been to confession in twenty-five years. Why would he go to confession if he didn't have nothing to confess, Freda, huh? You tell me, why?"

"I don't know," I said, "but it doesn't have to mean he's cheating. There's probably some other reason. Have you talked to him about it?"

At this point the rumpus flared up again. There was the sound of shrieking, maybe some blows being exchanged, a loud bang, and then the line went dead. I never found out exactly what happened, but shortly afterward my uncle and aunt finally got a phone installed in their apartment.

I was pretty sure Ninfa was wrong. Although I knew my uncle found her irritating at times, I really couldn't imagine him as the lover of someone else. I tried to picture him in a candle-lit restaurant toying with the fallen tresses of another woman; the two of them strolling hand in hand through the gardens of the Villa Borghese; him ripping off his baggy Y-fronts and leaping into her bed for a night of passion. It was no good. It didn't work. Uncle Birillo just wasn't the type to have a mistress.

Diverting as these thoughts were, I had my Pierino to consider, and he had to come first. So I dressed hurriedly and raced to the printers in the Via Santa Anna. There I wrote out a message and had it run off, fifty copies, offering a generous reward for the safe return of my parrot. Immediately, the printer's assistant and five of the seven customers told me they had found just such a bird, but I remained skeptical. I had to be wary of fraudsters.

Then, equipped with a reel of sticky tape, I wandered around posting my notices on statues, parked cars, posts, trees, and walls throughout the district.

"You see, she doesn't offer a reward for the return of the husband." I heard a voice and tittering behind me.

"I saw them take him, you know." It was the butcher, Carlo Martello. I joined the crowd that quickly gathered around him, and elbowed my way to the front.

"Yes, Signora Lippi," he continued, juggling a monstrous

flap of tripe in his hands, "I saw it all. There were seven, no eight assassins. I did what I could to save him, but they had guns, big guns, machine guns, in fact. I will never forget the look on his face as they bundled him into the back of the van and drove away. I will see it until my dying day . . ."

"That's garbage," interrupted Giangiacomo Campobasso, the hairdresser. "You saw nothing. I, I saw everything. There were only two of them. Both disguised as harlequins. There were no machine guns. One of them had a pistol, which he held to the back of Signor Lippi's head. He was forced into the trunk of a dark blue sedan, driven by a blond woman whose roots were in urgent need of attention . . ."

"The both of you are talking out of your bottoms," interrupted Manilia Pietrapertosa, the doll-sized woman who had run the lemon stall for the past sixty years. "They took him away in a helicopter."

"A hot-air balloon," shouted Fausto Pazzi.

"Gorilla suits. They were wearing gorilla suits," screamed Bernadetta Sorbolito.

"Helicopters. Harlequins. Gorillas. How many of those do you see round here?" asked Crispino Mongillo, trying to restore a note of sanity. But I had already walked away.

While I was still fixing up the notices, fifty-three people, including two sets of identical twins, three nuns, a violinist, four blind men, seventeen German tourists, and a woman with a bushy beard and matching dog, all claimed to have found Pierino. Zookeepers and pet store proprietors would need to beware.

Without meaning to, I found myself in the Via di Campo Marzio, where Alberto's mother lived in an apartment above the ecclesiastical outfitters, upstairs from his sister, Nunziata, and her children, currently numbering six. What strong genes were at work in that family. All of them short, fat, and upsettingly alike.

I offered up heartfelt thanks to the Virgin that I had managed to avoid what would have been an immaculate conception, and tiptoed past Nunziata's apartment. I could not face meeting her or her brood. Within, there were the sounds of mayhem: wailing and screaming, ripping cloth, shattering glass, brawling, singing, laughter, and caterwauling.

By contrast, upstairs was eerily quiet. Seeing Alberto's mother sitting there, still as a photograph of herself, with her hands folded in her lap, made me confront the reality of his disappearance for the first time. It could have been him sitting there with the white lace cap on his head and the heavy crystal earrings distorting the holes in her lobes.

The smell in the room was of her old age and rancor, decay mixed with something unpleasant but unspecific. That smell too Alberto shared in some measure.

There were lace doilies on every surface, and a great many items of basketwork, woven by the inmates of the San Cataldo *manicomio*. On the occasional table was a carton of miniature carrots made out of *pasta reale*. I remembered them from the first visit I made to the apartment, three years ago, when Signora Lippi urged Alberto not to marry me. Photographs of him, and Nunziata, and the grandchildren at various stages in their development stared at me from all around.

She recognized me, I knew. In the fragment of a second as I opened the door, her eyes, Alberto's eyes, were turned upon me. But now she was pretending not to know who I was.

"How are you, Signora Lippi?" I asked her, kissing her on both chubby cheeks. Her flesh was cold and hard like wax.

I had never been able to call her anything less formal than Signora Lippi.

"Signora Lippi, prepare yourself," I continued, although she had not acknowledged me. "I have some bad news. The worst possible news, in fact, about Alberto."

She didn't say anything, although I knew she was weighing my words. There was nothing wrong with her hearing. She had been known to eavesdrop on her neighbors at the far end of the street.

"He has been taken. Seized. Disappeared."

Her eyes didn't even flicker.

"Yes," I continued, "on Saturday, before he was due to appear at Berenice's. The police have little hope of his being found alive."

I garbled on, filling in the details, although she did nothing to encourage me. It was always this way. Around her I was seized by the urge to fill in all the spaces, not to leave any gaps for unpleasantness to fester.

Finally I ran out of things to say, like a clockwork toy run down. For a moment or two there was a vacuum. Then her thick lips twitched. Was she about to speak? I put all my strength into my ears. What would she say?

"Peas. Fresh peas."

"Peas?"

Then she relapsed into silence. When it became obvious there was nothing more to say, I left the apartment. I never wanted to see any of the Lippi clan again.

I jumped on a passing bus. I didn't especially care where it was going. The driver stared at me as though he recognized me from somewhere, but I couldn't place him. It was crowded, and I was squashed between overheated bodies. I wriggled along to escape the hot breath on the back of my neck, but then felt someone rubbing against my buttocks. I glared around me looking for the perpetrator, but it could have been any one of a number of people. One man nursing a crate of tomatoes kept winking, but I think he just had a bad case of conjunctivitis.

I got off at the next stop, making a mental note to myself never to travel by bus again. I stepped down outside a branch of the Banca di Roma and thought I may as well withdraw the reward money I was offering for Pierino's return.

"The short, fat man is on the run," said a man two ahead in the line to nobody in particular. "The short fat man is on the run," he repeated loudly.

"They say he has already undergone plastic surgery," said his neighbor, a woman with a magnificent hairy wart on one cheek.

"Yes, I've seen him," said a security guard. "He's been stretched and is now twice the size he was."

"The police are searching for a long thin man with severe stretch marks."

"Of course, the dummy isn't really a dummy at all."

"He's a spy wanted by Interpol."

I listened in a halfhearted way. It was quite a coincidence. The person they were talking about could almost have been Alberto. But of course it wasn't. Alberto wasn't wanted by the police. He certainly wasn't on the run. And, of course, Malco was a dummy—he lived in a suitcase under my bed—I ought to know.

Eventually, as those ahead of me got served, I reached the front of the line.

"I'd like to withdraw some cash," I said to the teller, handing her a check. She took one look at my name and sucked in her lips. Then she pressed the panic button under the desk.

The manager came forward to the bulletproof glass, and

he and the teller whispered something to each other. Then, the security guard seized my arm and I was propelled toward an office, where the manager soon appeared. Various members of the staff squeezed in behind him, together with some of the customers, a newspaper vendor, and a man with a tray of coffee cups. They stood in a line looking at me as if I were an exhibit.

"What is going on?" I demanded.

"Signora Lippi, you must be aware that your husband has absconded owing several millions to the bank?"

"Nonsense," I snapped, "Alberto Lippi [I couldn't bring myself to refer to him as 'my husband'] has been abducted. How can he owe you several millions?"

"The matter is in the hands of the police. If you are shielding him, you can expect to reap the consequences. Your bank account has been frozen."

"Brini," he said to the security guard, "please escort Signora Lippi off the premises. I will be right behind you, and if there is any trouble, rest assured, the police will be called."

"Just a minute—" I spluttered, but it was pointless. The guard seized my arm for the second time, and at a rapid pace I was ejected from the building like a common criminal, before I could say or do anything.

I was shaking with rage and mortification, and had to sit

down on a bench to calm myself. They were telling me Alberto was a fugitive from justice, and owed the bank millions. I just couldn't believe it. The Detective said Alberto had been seized. Why would he say that if it wasn't true? Now my bank account had been frozen. Mine! And I had only a few coins left in my purse. How would I pay the reward money for Pierino? People are so ruthless. There would be no charity. I didn't like to think what would happen to Pierino if I couldn't pay. Although I had never borrowed a cent in my life, I would have to ask Signora Dorotea for a loan.

I just didn't know what to think anymore. Admittedly, despite having been married to him for three years, I didn't know Alberto very well. Were he and this bandit one and the same?

I started walking. I thought I shouldn't waste money by taking a taxi; besides, I didn't have the cash to pay for one. As I walked, I thought everything over. I rummaged through the past looking for clues, signs, any hint at all that Alberto had been living a double life. Although nothing struck me as suspicious, I had to conclude that anything was possible. Those months when I thought he was away at sea he could have been up to all sorts of villainy. Only the dummy would know for sure, but I was certain he wouldn't tell me anything.

When I turned into the Via dei Cappellari, I was shocked

to see a line waiting outside my building, circling the block. There were a few policemen keeping order, and an enterprising soul was selling ice cream and cool drinks from a cart. As I got closer I recognized Cremoso, Fiamma's suitor from all those years ago. He flashed me his dazzling one-tooth smile and offered me a cone, which I declined. I saw then that the people in the queue were holding boxes, cages, and baskets. My heart performed a somersault. Maybe one of them had found Pierino.

I hadn't put my address on the flyer, quite deliberately, because of the numbers of perverts at large in the city, but somehow these people had found me anyway. I started with the first man, who was waiting patiently on the top step with an enormous cage covered by a patterned cloth.

"Have you found my parrot?" I asked him.

"It depends on how much you're prepared to pay for him," came his reply.

"I'll pay what's fair," I said. "First show me the bird."

Carefully he drew back the cover. At first I couldn't see anything in there. No bright blue feathers certainly. There was, however, something lying in the bottom of the cage. Was my Pierino ill? Hurt? I bent down and peered in, but it wasn't my parrot. It was a small rodent.

"Is this some kind of a joke?" I demanded. "I advertised for a parrot, not a rat."

"It's not a rat," said the man indignantly. "It's a hamster. And it can talk. Come on, Nino, say something."

"I will not," said the hamster archly. It had a deep voice, quite unlike the squeaky tone you might have expected.

"Fancy that," said the man second behind in the line, "a talking hamster; who'd have believed it, eh? How much do you want for him?"

"Fifty."

"I'll give you thirty."

"Forty, then."

"Done."

I felt suddenly redundant. I walked along the line looking for people with birdcages.

"Has anyone here got a parrot?" I asked loudly. "A real parrot, blue in color, answers to the name of Pierino."

A chorus of voices answered me, but my hopes were not high. After examining the contents of many cages, shoe boxes, egg boxes, jam jars, and paper bags, I counted eleven goldfish, seven performing rabbits, a Barbary ape, a singing centipede, a tap-dancing frog, four dogs with varying talents, a duck, and a snake. There was not one parrot among them.

Eventually, I lost hope. I could see they were a bunch of hustlers, out to make easy money by praying on people's misfortunes. I left them waiting there and locked myself in my apartment, from where I could still hear the barking and quacking and tap-dancing.

four

The first thing I did was to call the Detective. I had to know the truth about Alberto. Had he been seized? Or had he absconded? Was he a thief? Had I been duped, and made to look a fool?

As I waited for the Detective to answer, I became conscious of feeling hot and shivery. Soon I would hear his deep voice breathing "Balbini" into my ear. Except I didn't. After it rang for ages, his subordinate picked it up. He told me the Detective had just gone off duty, but would return my call in the morning. In the morning? I looked at my watch and was stunned to see it was already seven—where had the whole day gone?

Without the answers to these questions, I knew I would be in a lather all night. I strode into the bedroom ready to interrogate the dummy, but the case was empty. Now he too had gone. Suppose he wasn't really a dummy after all, but a midget, Alberto's accomplice? The idea was absurd, but so many ridiculous things were going on, maybe it wasn't that implausible after all. When I thought of all that Malco had witnessed between Alberto and me, it made my toes curl up. A third one in our marriage, he had always been there, right from the start. Though, to be more accurate, they were the couple, and I was the outsider.

I needed to speak to somebody, so I called Signora Dorotea.

"Freda, I've been worried about you," she said. "I thought you were coming in this afternoon. I've had two murders, a suicide, an industrial decapitation, a road traffic accident, and seven natural causes to deal with."

"I'm sorry," I said. "I have had the weirdest day," and I explained everything that had happened.

"It must be a mistake," she said reassuringly. "Alberto a bank robber! Never. He's far too stupid. Now, don't worry yourself about the money. There's any amount here for you; you only have to say the word."

I felt a bit better after speaking to Signora Dorotea. Over the years I suppose she had become almost a second mother to me.

Before long the phone rang. I was wary of answering in case it was a crazy person trying to sell me an imaginary parrot. I almost missed having Signor Tontini scream at me to answer it.

When I picked it up, it was Fiamma. "You're coming to a Lebanese Cultural and Chinese Trade evening. I've sent the car over for you. It will be there in ten minutes."

"Oh, no, not tonight," I said. "Some other time I'd love to . . ." but she had already hung up.

This wasn't the first time I had been invited to one of Fiamma's official functions. They were usually terribly boring. I think she did it to assuage her guilt about not seeing me enough, but of course while she was presiding over these banquets, she never had time to talk to me anyway.

If Pesco was on his way, I supposed I would have to go, although it was the last thing I felt like doing. Still, if I got the opportunity, I could try to consult with Fiamma about Alberto. Maybe she could pull a few strings in the Secret Service and find out just what was going on.

Before I even had time to pull a comb through my hair, I saw the limousine squeeze into my street and pull up in front of the Belbo Forno. I fought my way through the crowd outside which had swelled to include a gypsy band offering a mule, a brightly colored iguana, and a piglet.

Fiamma and Polibio had long since left the apartment in the Via della Lupo. Now they occupied a palazzo in the Via del Corso that went with Fiamma's job. They lived in the lap of luxury amid marble corridors; state rooms adorned with frescoes, gold leaf, and giant candelabra; and, naturally, a retinue of servants on call at all hours.

Pesco, whose mother was having the customary trouble with her hemorrhoids, dropped me off at the kiosk outside the palace, where I was frisked by a security agent.

"She's clear," he said into a walkie-talkie, whereupon a disheveled maid with wild eyes and a pair of powerful calves swung open the great front door.

First to greet me was Polibio junior, now aged three, who was wearing a top hat, and a flowing cloak over his pajamas. Although I had only just arrived, his greatest wish was to make me disappear, but his elementary magic kit couldn't rise to the challenge. The child was frighteningly like his father, inheriting along with his love of conjuring tricks and bad jokes, a craving for pickles.

Polibio senior then appeared and handed me a glass of his rum punch, which gave off a vapor like smoke. Suspecting one of his pranks, I looked for somewhere to pour it.

In the grandest reception room, admiring the objets d'art, was a tall man who had his back to me. When he turned around, I found myself face-to-face with the Detective. I gasped, and dropped my glass, which shattered on the mosaic floor. Some of its contents landed on my foot and I could feel burning.

"Well, Max, you certainly made an impression on her!" said Polibio, pinching my cheek, and then poking his finger in my ear.

Max! What funny business was going on here? Immediately the maid appeared, handed me another glass of the smoking punch, and cleared away all traces of the one I had just dropped.

"Freda Lippi, my old friend Max Calderone; Max, Freda, Freda, Max." Polibio gave an obvious wink and nudge to his "friend" and ostentatiously withdrew from the room, leaving the two of us together.

"What's going on?" I whispered. "What are you doing here? Why are you using an alias?"

He put his finger to his lips, urging me to silence, but I needed answers.

"Is it true that Alberto is a fugitive from justice and owes millions to the bank?"

"Are you aware your shoe is melting?" he countered, and it was true, the patent leather was curling up and dying a painful death.

Fiamma buzzed in, between urgent phone calls, to greet us.

"Max, how good to see you again. It's been a long time." She kissed him on either cheek. She was playing her part well. "Fredina—dressed ready for a funeral, I see. We're just waiting for a few others. The prime minister can't make it, but the Lebanese cultural attaché and the Chinese trade delegation will be here shortly."

Immediately, Fiamma's secretary came to summon her, and she hurried out again.

"Is it true?" I hissed at the Detective. "I have to know."

He pulled his earlobe, and then gestured toward the open door. I didn't know what was going on, but I was getting more and more frustrated. Why wouldn't he answer me?

"Is the dummy wanted by Interpol?" I insisted.

"Charming room," he said, helping himself to a glass of the noxious punch. Without thinking, I tipped mine into the pot containing the massive rubber plant that had been in Polibio's family for five generations. It was a big mistake. The soil hissed and bubbled, and I watched in horror as the leaves at the bottom began to wither; then the next layer up did the same. The contagion spread through the trunk and along the branches. In a matter of seconds all that was left was a smoking skeleton and a pile of dead leaves.

The Detective nodded to the long damask drapes framing

the windows, and together we took hold of the massive pot and dragged it where it would be hidden from view. On our hands and knees we gathered up the fallen leaves. There were hundreds of them, and they were so hot they burned my hands. At this point there was the sound of a squeaky wheel, footsteps, and incomprehensible chattering in the foyer. The luminaries were on their way.

I opened my bag, and frantically we thrust the leaves inside. Thankfully I had brought the big one with fifteen compartments ("for the woman who likes to be organized," as it said in the advertisement). I had never liked it. We were just getting up from the floor when Polibio rode in on his unicycle. Following behind him were the foreign dignitaries, the simultaneous translators, and the senior civil servants.

"Hello, hello," he said, dismounting and handing the cycle to the maid. "At it already? Now, gentlemen, here's that card trick I promised you . . ."

Polibio was a buffoon. Already I was feeling much less bad about the rubber plant.

Later I heard him saying to Fiamma:

"They were on the floor, I tell you."

"Shhhh, they'll hear you."

"Your sister's a fast one; there is no mistake about it. She was on top of him. If I hadn't gone in when I did . . ."

At dinner I was seated between two of the Chinese businessmen. There weren't enough translators to go round, so we smiled and nodded a lot. I tried to mime what I did for a living, but I don't think they understood. The one to my left built an elaborate structure out of fruit and then stabbed at it with a knife. The other one pursed his lips and made a rich variety of animal noises. It was fascinating.

Across from me, on the other side of the wide table, sat the Detective. All the time I could feel his dark eyes on me. I wondered at first if it was because I had spilled some of the tomato sauce down my front, but when I took a look, I couldn't see any. I began to feel warm and sticky, and was pleased when the intermezzo was served—a refreshing pear sorbet arranged in little dishes made of ice.

At this point I noticed there were wisps of smoke coming from my purse: the leaves were still smoldering. I poured a jug of water in and snapped the clasp shut. Assuming it was a local custom, the Chinese businessmen opened up their briefcases and filled them with water. Then we nodded and smiled.

Soon I felt my legs being caressed under the table. The lightest whisper of a touch running up the insides of my calves. I wondered if it was Polibio playing a joke, but he was far away at the other end of the long table. I began to squirm in my seat, feeling hot and damp inside. Taking their cue from me, my neighbors began wriggling too. Opposite, the Detective never removed his eyes from me, and the hint of a smile played upon his lips.

Under these circumstances, I hardly even noticed the hour of speeches given in Arabic and Mandarin, and all too soon the banquet was breaking up. Fiamma was already aboard a helicopter bound for Brussels, so I wasn't able to broach the subject of Alberto. Neither did I have the opportunity to speak to the Detective again, for by the time I had completed the elaborate farewell ritual with my businessmen, he had disappeared. With their briefcases dripping trails of inky water, they rejoined their delegation on the tour bus, and I climbed into the waiting limousine for Pesco to drive me home.

Thankfully the carnival of animals had moved on by the time he deposited me outside my building. In the hallway was the lingering smell of smoke, and the communal light wasn't working. I had come to dread what I would find whenever I came home. In total darkness, I felt my way up the stairs.

Outside the door to my apartment, a figure was lurking. I froze, stifling a scream. Who was it? What did he want? Then the flame from a cigarette lighter illuminated the scarred face of Dario Mormile, the proprietor of the Berenice cabaret club.

"Freda," he hissed out of the side of his mouth. "Don't turn on the lights. They could be watching me."

"Who?" I whispered back.

"Don't ask me any questions. I know you need money. Take this." He shoved a number of folded bills into my hand. "It's okay, take it; think of it as what was owed to Alberto. You need a way to earn some extra cash, right? I got a job for you. Hatcheck. At the club. No strings. Come by tomorrow. Don't say nothing to nobody."

With that he slithered down the staircase like a snake, keeping flat against the wall.

Although I had left every window open, Pierino had still not returned. I climbed into bed fully clothed and pulled the covers over my head. I just needed the whole of today to go away.

five

On my way to work the following morning I actually saw Alberto some distance ahead of me on the sidewalk. I recognized him immediately. Like someone I had known a long time ago in a different life. Already a gulf separated us. Although it had only been three days, he seemed smaller and fatter than I remembered. He was wearing the gold lamé suit that had gone missing from his closet, and, strangely, he had the hairpiece on his head, although I was sure that it was still in the apartment. How could I have married him? I asked myself, aghast. How could I have slept in the same bed with him? How had I endured (albeit only once or twice) those things that never should have happened?

Clearly he wasn't in the clutches of the Mafia. So was he a bank robber? I had to know. I started running, dodging between the early morning ranks of trainee priests, nuns, vegetable vendors, office workers, hairdressers, and acrobats. Suppose he offered to come back? What then? My pace slowed momentarily as I pondered this thought. But then I speeded up again. This was the perfect opportunity to tell him I wanted a divorce.

I gained on him and reached out, taking hold of his costume at the back. It ripped. When he turned around, it wasn't Alberto at all. It was another man entirely, and he was furious that I held the back panel of his suit jacket in my hand.

"Attack," he screamed. "Help. Police. Murder."

A crowd was quick to gather.

"I'm sorry," I shouted. "I mistook you for someone else. Take this—" I thrust at him, along with the piece of his jacket, one of the notes given me by Dario Mormile. "This should cover the cost of repairs."

But the man screamed on, "Assault. Battery. Mayhem."

How typical that I should run into a maniac.

Then others in the crowd started shouting:

"You can rip my jacket for thirty."

"Twenty-five."

"Twenty and I'll throw in the cravat for free."

I ran away across the Via del Pellegrino, my pulse racing. I was no nearer to discovering the truth, and today was set to be as crazy as yesterday. As I stumbled into the Via Sora, I heard the flutter of wings. Not any old flutter. A distinctive flutter that I immediately recognized. I looked around, and sure enough, Pierino was just above me, clinging to a stone scallop on the side of the building. My heart sang. If only I could catch him.

"Pierino!" I shrilled. "Come here, come on, come to Mamma." He looked at me, winked, and flapped lazily away toward the Palazzo del Governo. I ran after him, dodging the cars, mopeds, buses, and pony carts in search of early tourists. There was a great deal of cursing, gesticulating, and hooting of horns. I ignored it. My only thought was to get my Pierino back.

He flapped on at a steady pace, and every so often he looked round to check if I was still there. Like this we went along the Via di Parione and continued north. Then, in the Via della Pace, he suddenly swooped onto the railing of a balcony and began a systematic preening of his plumage.

I called him and called him, stretching out my arms and making the clucking and sucking noises with my lips that I knew he loved above all others. Although I could see he was enjoying my display, he still wouldn't come to me. After making a massive dropping, which splattered down onto the sidewalk by my feet, he ducked inside the open window.

I chose the lower bell by the front door and buzzed on it loudly, then stood back and worked out what I was going to say. After a while, the door opened and a little old woman appeared whose head was sparsely furnished with hair. She seemed annoyed.

"What do you want?" she demanded. "I don't want any rosaries, lottery tickets, lucky charms, love potions, or marshmallows, I tell you that now . . ."

"I'm from the ornithological society," I lied, flashing my library card at her and putting it away quickly before she could study it. "A rare parrot has just entered this building and by the powers invested in me by the State I am obliged to pursue it."

I pushed past her and ran up the stairs. There was a door on the upper landing, and I hammered on it. Eventually it opened a crack and a nose poked through. I barged my way in. The nose belonged to a woman who was now flattened behind the door. She peeled herself off the wall like a cartoon character and stood facing me. She looked for all the world like a ventriloquist's dummy. She had a painted face with two rouged spots in the center of her cheeks, shiny wooden hair, unnaturally pink limbs, and a stiff way of walking, as though her joints had seized.

"Just what is going on here?" I demanded. "You've got my

parrot. I saw him fly in through the window. Where is he? I'm taking him back."

Her jaw dropped following the grooves that led from her mouth down to her chin. No sound emerged but she clip-clopped in a wooden way down the passage and into the room beyond. I followed.

"There is no parrot here," she said at last, with a motion of her squeaky arms. I had heard that voice before; I knew I had. I had heard it in the dead of night, in my own bedroom. It was one of the voices that simpered with Alberto, and it made me shiver.

I scrutinized every corner of the room. She was right. There was no sign of Pierino. Without asking her leave, I walked around the apartment, looking into cupboards, under tables, on lampshades: there was not a hint that Pierino had been there. Not a feather. No droppings. No half-chewed fruit. The air was still—without a rumple. Although I could have sworn I saw him enter, I must have been wrong.

In a bedroom I found a swollen baby sleeping in a crib. It was the image of a baby Alberto, and the other Lippi off-spring. This one also had waxy red cheeks and what looked like painted-on hair.

"Is this Alberto's child?" I demanded.

She shook her head violently, and her neck produced such

a lavish selection of squeaks I though her ears were likely to fly off.

From the passage a voice was calling. It was the old woman from the lower floor.

"Genoveffa," she began.

Genoveffa, the name struck a chord with me. Many times I had heard Alberto whisper it in the dark.

"Have you got any parrots in here? If so you must surrender them to the authorities. It's against the terms of the lease, and we don't want an investigation, do we now?"

"If you have been secreting the parrot," I snapped on my way out, "you can expect an extremely thorough investigation by the authorities. They will leave no stone unturned, believe me." With that I walked down the steps and into the street.

Strangely the dropping that Pierino had deposited on the sidewalk had disappeared, and I began to ask myself if I was going mad.

That day at work was memorable because we had a miracle, and they didn't often happen. When we removed Mafalda Firpotto from the cold storage area and uncovered her withered body, we found a fine carpet of violets growing upon it. Signora Dorotea, who had seen many things during the course of her long career, threw her arms into the air shouting:

"It's a miracle. A miracle, Freda. Porzio, come quickly. Calipso, come and look."

Signor Porzio hurried in, and immediately dropped to his knees and began crossing himself. Behind him was Calipso Longo, the receptionist, who collapsed and had to be brought round with smelling salts.

"By the grace of the Madonna," she gurgled. "Truly it is a miracle."

I didn't know much about miracles, but it was certainly strange. From a scientific point of view, it shouldn't have been possible, but I examined Mafalda Firpotto closely and saw with my own eyes the violets growing out of her flesh. They covered her torso and meandered along her arms and legs, where they culminated in a flourish on her hands and feet.

Immediately Signora Dorotea put in a call to the Santa Fosca convent, where Mafalda Firpotto, a widow, had spent her last years immersed in prayer and contemplation, in the care of the sisters. While Signora Dorotea was still speaking, the sisters piled into their antiquated minibus, driven by the mother superior, Sister Prisca, and hurtled toward the center of the city from their convent in the suburbs.

We worked fast to arrange Mafalda Firpotto in a fine mahogany coffin, and then propelled her into a chapel of rest, where the chairs were set out neatly in rows, and the music of a harp drifted gently over the public address system. Immediately the air became suffused with the sweet scent of violets, magnified to an extraordinary intensity, and, skeptical as I was, I couldn't help but feel a sense of astonishment.

Somehow the news had traveled, and in no time the reception area was filled with onlookers. The bloodstained butchers from the adjoining shop had rushed in with the hairdressers and bedraggled customers from the salon on the other side. Ballerinas, firemen, zookeepers, melon vendors, rat catchers, schoolboys, priests, and tailors pushed their way in behind. There was even a juggler and a clown from the Circo Ippolito, who just happened to be passing. Calipso Longo, enjoying her moment of glory, kept the crowd behind a cordon and maintained order with a ruler.

When the sisters arrived, they were ushered into the chapel of rest, and immediately they prostrated themselves before the coffin, hailed Mafalda Firpotto as a saint, pronounced the phenomenon of the growing violets a miracle, and claimed for their convent the glory associated with it. Their priest, Padre Bonifacio, held an impromptu mass, and then a press conference for the many journalists and television crews that had gathered in the staff room.

Among them I recognized my old friend the photographer from *Mortician's Monthly,* and we were to feature on the front page of the August issue. More exciting still, Signora Dorotea and I were actually interviewed by Channel One and we appeared on the television in a news bulletin. Aunt Ninfa was so excited by my moment of fame that she threw a party for the neighbors, and brought in a selection of *pizzetti* and opened a bottle of wine. Although our item was over in seven seconds, and, naturally, given her garrulous nature, Signora Dorotea did most of the talking, still Aunt Ninfa basked in my reflected luster for ages afterward, and felt, for the first time since her suspicions of Birillo's infidelity were aroused, that she could hold her head up high in the district.

At five I slipped away, because it was impossible to get any work done in the mayhem caused by the miracle, and besides, there was other business demanding my attention. I had the idea of taking myself down to the area by the station where the most unsavory characters in the city lurked. There, it was widely known, you could find escaped convicts, cutthroats, pirates, itinerant assassins, underworld gangs, mercenaries, and, naturally, the most merciless mafiosi. I would ask a few questions—see what I could find out.

In order to get on with my life, I had to know that Alberto wouldn't be coming back. If I could be sure he had been disappeared, and was now forming the foundations of some multistory parking garage or *autostrada* on stilts, I could stop worrying. Did that make me callous? Possibly. But as you know, ours was no love match, and I couldn't spend the rest of my life trying to make sense of his disappearance.

In the Piazza dei Cinquecento, in front of the "*dinosauro,*" I spotted an unpleasant individual with a festering scar on his cheek, and a checkered cap that I thought marked him out as a member of a gang.

I approached him cautiously.

"Have you seen the ventriloquist?" I began.

He narrowed his eyes and exhaled a slow plume of smoke. "I saw a puppet show once when I was a kid. Why?"

"I mean the short, fat man. Do you know anything?"

"Let's see," he said, taking a long drag on his cigarette. "Is he this short?" And he gestured with his hand the exact height of Alberto.

"Yes!"

"And is he, say, this fat?" He held his hands out wide and jiggled them up and down.

"Yes!" I said again, feeling I was getting somewhere. "That's right."

"Never seen him," and with that he sidled away, eyeing me like a maniac.

Deflated, I walked on looking for someone who looked dangerous, but at the same time, sensible. It wasn't easy—the two didn't seem to go together. I discounted a man surrounded by a swarm of bluebottles, an accordion player with a vicious-looking monkey, and a bogus priest—one of the thousands that thronged the city—who was brandishing a machete. Finally I approached a man in a dark suit with a violin case and bandy legs.

"I'm seeking information on a short, fat ventriloquist called Alberto Lippi," I said.

"I'm sorry, I'm late for a recital," he replied, and hurried away in the direction of the Teatro dell' Opera.

"Can you tell me anything about the short, fat man?" I asked a greasy man with a liver-colored dog.

"Yes," he said. "A flying saucer took him away, and now he's the leader of the aliens."

It was hopeless. I wasn't getting anywhere. I suppose I had been foolish even to try. Still, it was time for me to head to the Berenice for my first night in the cloakroom. If I kept my eyes and ears open, I might yet learn something useful.

The Berenice club was in the Via Vittoria, sandwiched between the taxidermist (to my overwhelming relief there were no parrots on display) and the surgical corset makers (satisfaction guaranteed). It was down in a basement reached by narrow steps, above which hung a blinking blue lantern. The air outside had the reek of a public urinal, the sidewalk was smeared with disgusting detritus, and in the gutter lay a drunk sighing, "Mona, Mona," between bursts of anguished groaning.

A number of shy and spotty seminarians clustered around the entrance, trying to summon up the courage to go inside. The door was blocked by a hulking man in a too-tight suit. His neck was wider than his head, and his bottom lip protruded as though it wanted no part of him.

"I have an appointment with Signor Mormile," I said to the hulk.

His lump of a lip flexed to show acknowledgment, and he moved slightly, ever so slightly, to one side, but not enough to allow me to get past him easily. I had to squeeze through the tiny gap that remained between where he finished and the doorframe began, and his body and mine seemed to combine intimately in the time it took.

Inside the club it was dark and dirty. The air was weighted down by stale cigarette smoke, and I recognized the sick smell of rotting meat emanating from what I presume was the kitchen. My feet stuck to the floor, and the soles were almost torn from my shoes as I attempted to walk. This was the third pair I had ruined in less than a week. The red flock wallpaper was badly worn, and the portrait of the club's founder, the stocky Berenice, hung at a drunken angle and had been adorned with a beard, mustache, and spectacles. It was a very different establishment from the ones where Mamma used to work.

Music was playing, and heading toward it, I ducked through a beaded curtain into the saloon itself. A spotlight came on, illuminating a figure in a tight red dress standing on a small stage at the back of the room. At first glance it seemed to be a woman, but one with the body of a man. Her shoulders were too wide, her neck too thick, and her hands and feet were enormous. There was a ripple of applause as she was introduced as "Miss Olga Mollica."

She began to sing, "Sempre Tu," and I have to say she had a good voice, even if it was rather deep.

I stumbled around the room looking for Dario Mormile. It was so dark that I could make out only the glowing ends of many cigarettes. I could vaguely detect figures moving about, and as my eyes adjusted I saw they were dancing. There must have been a shortage of women, because the couples were mostly men dancing together. There were a number of tables dotted about with figures seated at them. Two men seemed to be having an argument, although not much could be heard above the sound of Miss Mollica and the band. The blade of a knife flashed a gleam of light, and one of the men ran out holding a handkerchief to his cheek.

"Dance?" drooled a voice in my ear, but luckily the owner of the voice then fell down in a heap at my feet. I stepped over him and made for the exit. Too late though. Before I could make my escape, I saw Mormile coming toward me.

"I think I'll go," I said, trying to smile.

He came up close. Too close, and placed his hand on my neck. For one horrible moment I thought he was going to kiss me.

"I need you, Freda," he said in a low voice. I felt his breath on my face, and it smelled like a sneaker. "I can't rely on any of the others. They're all leaving me. Walking out. Rats leaving a sinking ship. There for the good times, but when times are hard, they're out the door. But you, Freda, you ain't like the other girls." Here his hand began to stray round to the nape of my neck, and toy with my hair. "You want to help Dario, don't you, Freda?"

I didn't, but I didn't know how to say so. I had always felt bad about saying no.

"Terrific," he said, interpreting my momentary silence as affirmation. "Here's what you do . . ." He took me by the hand and led me to a filthy booth at the end of the corridor that was equipped with a rail of coat hangers, an artificial geranium, and a book of raffle tickets.

As he sidled away, rubbing himself against his own flock wall paper (perhaps he alone was responsible for the wear and tear), he turned and called back:

"You sing, Freda?"

I shook my head quickly.

"Good girl," he said with a wink.

The doorman walked past with the neck of the drunken dancer in his hand, swinging him like a chicken. I stood awkwardly in the booth trying not to breathe too much because of the stench, thinking—as I had on my wedding night—"What on earth am I doing here?" A few customers filtered through. Mechanically I took their hats and issued them with tickets. When Uncle Birillo came in with a lady in pink, we both got the shock of our lives.

"Office party," he said quickly by way of explanation, handing me his fedora.

"Shall I keep the stole and the hat together?" I asked, like a real cloakroom attendant.

"Oh, we're not together," he replied, sounding shocked at my mistake. "Oh, no. I've never seen this lady before," and with that he snatched up his ticket and strode into the saloon alone.

Poor Uncle Birillo. He always worked such long hours. Even his evenings were spent with clients and colleagues. The Goloso Gas and Oil Company seemed to own him, body and soul.

"If I could only be sure Alberto was dead," I confided to Signora Dorotea the following morning as I sculpted a nose out of wax for Signora Agnello (her own had been eaten by a goat as she lay dying); "then I could get on with my life. It's not knowing that's driving me crazy."

"Leave it to me, Freda," she replied with a wink. "I'll put out word to the Guild and see if somebody can help us. Who knows? One of the brethren could have buried him." With that she bustled into her office, applied her pince-nez to her nose, and consulted the sacred leather-bound ledger that she kept locked in the safe.

The Guild was, of course, the secretive society formed by the city's undertakers. Membership was fiercely guarded, and was passed down strictly along family lines. Signora Dorotea was, naturally, high up in the Guild, reflecting her unparalleled pedigree in the business. She had held every office in her time, including Grand Mistress (twice), and she took her duties seriously, attending every conclave and convocation, to which she wore a blue cape embroidered with moons and stars, a jeweled turban, and carried a miniature trowel.

She spent most of the morning on the phone, while I finished crafting the nose, glued it on, and then finished Signora Agnello's makeup and hairdo. When we returned from a quick lunch at Pirillo's (*penne alla carbonara, pollo in padella, fragole*), there was a message waiting, the contents of which Signora Dorotea announced jubilantly to me:

"The Buco twins in Salario may have him in their cold storage. They're burying him at five, so there's no time to lose."

With that we grabbed our purses, ran out into the Corso, and hailed a taxi.

Inexplicably the driver seemed determined to take us on a scenic tour of the city. He made a detour past the Trevi Fountain, and when he asked whether we would like to take in the Spanish Steps, Signora Dorotea took from her bag her ornamental trowel and hit him sharply on the head with it.

"Take us straight to the Via Ombrone," she hissed, "and no more monkey business."

At four-twenty-seven we leapt out of the taxi in front of the *portone* that led to the Buco's premises.

"Now, Freda," said Signora Dorotea, taking hold of my arm, "there's one thing you've got to be prepared for before we go in." She paused for effect and her eyes bulged. "The head's missing."

Although it is true to say that I had tried to look at Alberto's body as little as possible during our marriage, yet I was still hopeful of making a positive identification of it.

We let ourselves through the doorway, and walked down the cobbled alleyway to the workshop at the rear. The heaps of rubbish in the yard, scrap metal, broken bottles, old boots, decaying sacks; the battered hearse; the flea-bitten nag with a faded black plume still set in his mane; the carriage with its axel broken; the pitiful mongrel chained in a corner; the feral cat searching for scraps among the ruins. All showed that this establishment was at the other end of the scale from the Onoranze Funebri Pompi.

At our approach, the twins (who were completely identical, down to their bushy black beards, protruding teeth, and nervous blinking) hurried out to greet us, rubbing the grease from their hands on their aprons and smoothing down their hair as though they were being presented to royalty.

Signora Dorotea made the elaborate bow, the sequence of footsteps, and the special two-handed handshake that Guild members customarily exchange, and did what she could to put the brothers at their ease.

"Now, my lads," she said, as they led us inside with much bowing and signaling of trowels that all three had taken out, "what information do you have on this poor headless fellow?"

"Not much," replied the twins in unison.

"He was left outside last night," said one.

"No sign of the head," said the other.

"Wearing funny clothes, he was."

"That's right, like some kind of a fancy dress costume."

At this Signora Dorotea and I exchanged hopeful glances. By this point we had arrived at what passed here for cold storage facilities. In reality it was an antiquated chest freezer with "Angelini Gelati," stenciled on the outside in faded gold letters.

The twins threw open the lid, exposing the headless body to view. It was a little squashed up, there not being sufficient room inside the freezer for it to lie out flat. The most striking thing about it was that it was covered with a thick matting of dark hair, like a coconut. Also it was muscular, not fat and flabby, although the height was about right. Details like the tattoo on the right forearm of a broken heart with "Cunegonda" written above, the size of the feet (enormous), and the scar from an old bullet wound on the left side of the belly: all confirmed my initial feeling that this was not Alberto. It was a bitter blow.

I shook my head and turned away.

We refused the twins' kind offer of an ice-cream, thanked them for their help and their time, and after another ritual of parting, we left them.

"Don't be downhearted, *bella*," said the signora, patting my hand as we sat in the taxi in the jam at the Piazza Fiume. "You never know what tomorrow may bring."

But it was hard for me to feel optimistic.

nine

That evening, despite the disappointment of the afternoon, I returned to Berenice's, which, I was to see in retrospect, was a big mistake. I didn't want to go back, and had told myself I wouldn't, but stupidly, very stupidly, I felt I couldn't let Mormile down.

The club was busier than the previous night, and there was a procession of customers checking things at the booth. And they weren't just hats either. The space I had available was soon filled with items I wouldn't have expected people to take with them to a cabaret club. I issued tickets on a garden spade, a mannequin dressed in a fur coat, an urn of ashes bearing a plaque that read, "Fingers," and a live lobster with its claws bound by rubber bands.

I was in the process of trying to arrange this stuff in the

tiny space, and had to keep getting it out and repacking it in a way that I thought was better, when I turned to find Dario Mormile right behind me. I jumped. I was shocked by his appearance. His left ear was heavily bandaged this time, and his arm was in a sling. He bore the look of a man in a state of desperation, and his bloodshot eyes betrayed a fear that made me feel almost sorry for him.

"Freda, I need your help," he croaked. He seemed to have lost his voice. "None of the acts have shown up tonight. Not a single one. Even Olga Mollica. His wife won't allow him out of the house. It's a conspiracy. They're trying to put me out of business." He ran the free flabby hand over his face, and I noticed it was shaking. "I know who's behind it too, and I'm going to get even." Now something of the old fire returned to his eyes and voice as he patted the bulging pocket of his greasy jacket.

"How can you be a cabaret club with no cabaret, Freda, I ask you? No acts, no punters," he continued, "They'll go to Fifi's or the Pussy Cat Lounge. I'll be ruined. So I need you to go on, Freda."

"Go on?" I asked stupidly.

"Terrific," he said. "I knew you'd do it. You're a talented girl. Who knows, this could be the making of you. Get yourself kitted out in the star's dressing room. Something sexy.

You're on in five minutes. The band knows the numbers; you just got to sing along."

"Oh, and, Freda," he added, "it would help if you could dance a little, just wiggle your hips. You got great hips. And feel free to use any of the props. The snake always knocks their socks off." With that he retreated into his office and the door slammed behind him.

I left the coat-check booth unattended—hopefully the items would be safe—and hurried to the star's dressing room, which was adjacent to the kitchen. It was more like a cupboard than a room, dingily lit by a bare bulb, and smelled of stale sweat and greasepaint. The walls were lined with pegs from which hung an array of garish costumes, feather boas, hats, wigs, parasols, and gloves, and the floor was strewn with shoes and theatrical props: angels' wings, whips, potted plants.

I didn't know where to begin, but I had to be fast. I selected a long blue sequined dress that I thought might look all right, and stripped off my clothes. Something made me feel that I was being watched, and as I turned I saw the door was ajar and a number of eyes at different heights were peeping in. I slammed it shut, unleashing cries of pain from the outside.

Then someone knocked loudly and shouted, "Freda Lippi. You're on in two minutes."

Two minutes! I threw on the dress. It didn't exactly fit, but it would have to do. It had a plunging neckline and a slit running up the thigh. I rummaged for some shoes in a pile and, in doing so, disturbed a snake that must have been sleeping in there. It was black, shiny, and angry. It reared up, hissed angrily, and spat at me. I felt a sharp and searing pain like a needle in my leg. The snake had bitten me! I just had to hope it wasn't poisonous. If Mormile thought I was going to appear with that vicious creature, he could think again. I examined the wound. It was circular and smoking.

"One minute!" shouted the voice again.

I climbed into a pair of silver shoes that were several sizes too big, slung a feather boa around my neck, stuck a wax flower in my hair, and slathered some red greasepaint on the apples of my cheeks to give myself the color my fear had taken away. Looking in the cracked mirror, I felt I made a passable show of being a cabaret singer.

"You're on," shouted the voice, and this time the door opened. The hulking doorman, who had a plaster stretched across his bloodied nose, reached in and took me firmly by the arm as if he had orders not to let me get away. I felt wobbly and struggled to keep my balance in the shoes. Stage fright, I guess.

I was escorted to the beaded curtain, where we stood waiting. My heart was beating irregularly and I could feel my face burning. Inside, Mormile himself was at the microphone addressing the customers in his croaky voice that was amplified to an unbearable loudness.

"Ladies and gentlemen, girls and boys, fresh from the world's luxury cruise liners where she—" Here he was interrupted by the microphone emitting a long and extremely painful whistle, but he carried on unheeding. "—and the fleshpots of Damascus, I ask you to give a warm and appreciative welcome to the beautiful and talented Signora Veronique Kapoor." There was a drum roll and then the band struck up the introduction to "L'Uomo Che Amo."

The spotlight picked out the door where I was waiting. The doorman thrust a microphone into my hand and shoved me through the curtain. In the glare I was totally blinded. I knew I had to start singing. Fortunately I knew the number well. My voice came, amplified and distorted beyond all recognition. It was as though someone else entirely was singing.

The white circle of the spotlight began to move slowly across the saloon and I knew I had to follow it, concentrating hard to stay in both the dress, which was trying hard to fall off, and the shoes. Mounting the steps to the little stage was particularly tricky, and I tripped more than once but hoped nobody would notice.

Once I was on the stage, I began to relax, and strange as it seems, I actually began to enjoy myself. Before I even reached the end of the first number, the applause was overwhelming. Seamlessly the band led straight into "Notte e Giorno," and I gave it my all.

"Freda, you're a star," shouted Mormile from beside the stage. And I felt like one too.

I sang my way through "Amante di Miei Sogni," swaying in time to the music, and even ventured to slide one of my legs out of the split in the skirt. Everything was going so well until I felt suddenly and unbearably hot and my legs gave way beneath me.

I fell off the stage and landed on something hard. The band members didn't know whether to play on or not; some did, some didn't, and the microphone, which I was still clutching, continued to amplify and broadcast my own panting breath. It felt like ages before the lights went on, and when they did, I was dazed.

I found I had landed on a table, extinguishing the candle and breaking the glasses. My head was in the lap of the owner of a white suit. I thought I was delirious when I saw the man wearing the suit: yes, it was the Detective again. In disguise, but there was no mistaking him, despite the obvious wig in the style of Elvis Presley, the fake suntan, and heavy gold jewelry.

"Freda," he gasped, "are you all right?"

"She's fine," said Mormile, who had appeared at my side. "The show must go on."

He clicked the fingers of his good hand in the direction of the band and then tried to haul me up. It was no good, my body just wouldn't respond. My tongue expanded and was heavy and furry like a gerbil.

"Snakebite," I managed to get out with what felt like my final breath.

The women in the audience started to scream, the men joined in, and there was a frantic scramble for the exit. In the ensuing panic evening dresses were ripped, silver shoes discarded, and hairpieces became dislodged.

"Poisonous snakes!" cried the patrons.

"Look out, there's a purple man-eating cobra."

"It's a boa constrictor."

"Rattlesnakes."

Tables were knocked over, and fires were started as candles ignited the upholstery. Soon the saloon was thick with a choking black smoke.

The band joined the exodus, and Franco got his double bass stuck in the doors. The customers continued pushing and shoving behind him, and eighteen people were injured in the crush. It was chaos. Mormile was running about trying to calm things down, but he only succeeded in making them worse. Finally he was silenced when he got his head stuck in the bell of a bass tuba.

Meanwhile, before I lost consciousness, I was aware of the Detective ripping off his jacket and wig. Surely he couldn't have romance on his mind at a time like this? No, instead he took hold of my injured leg and examined it closely. Then, taking out an enormous switchblade, he said:

"Freda, this might hurt a bit," and applied the blade to the wound.

The pain was terrible. I considered fainting but decided I would do better to remain alert. Then, when he had finished probing with the knife, he applied his lips to my leg and started sucking. He sucked and sucked again, and then, periodically, spat the contents of his mouth vigorously onto the floor. I was worried I would be sucked dry. The smoke was so thick by this time our eyes were streaming and it was difficult to breathe.

Alerted by the chaos of the patrons fleeing the building and the smoke pouring out, the police took the opportunity of mounting a raid on the club they had been keeping under surveillance for several years. A squadron of uniformed officers rushed in waving batons. One started to beat the Detective violently on the head and body.

"Taking advantage of an injured woman," said the sergeant with contempt, amid the raining blows, "you ought to be ashamed of yourself. Take that!" The Detective, beaten to a state of unconsciousness, fell on top of me. This was the point at which I definitely blacked out.

I felt a splash of something cold over my face and opened my eyes to find the slow-melting eyes of the Detective looking into them anxiously.

"Madonna be praised," he said. "Freda, you pulled through." His voice was plump with emotion, betraying that his feelings for me were more than strictly professional.

My eyes stung a bit, and I located a slice of lemon on my upper lip and a few ice cubes in my cleavage. The gin and tonic had brought me round, where all else had failed. The Detective lifted me into a chair. His arms were strong and muscular, and I felt weightless as a doll in them.

The flames had been extinguished by the doorman, who was now using his jacket to beat out the final smolders from the upholstery. As the smoke cleared, the patrons began to file back in ones and twos. The members of the band unblocked the doorway. Franco got his double bass unstuck, but it was badly splintered and two of the strings were broken. Selmo d'Angelo managed to prize his bass tuba from Dario Mormile's head, but only by lying behind him on the floor, and jamming his feet on Mormile's shoulders for leverage.

They regrouped themselves, and struck up a swinging rendition of "Per Favore Credimi." One or two couples, including some of the police officers, who had resheathed their batons, took to the floor and began to dance. Beata Fresca, the waitress, was suddenly run off her feet as orders for drinks flooded in. Everybody needed to calm down and cool off. I was shocked to find my injured thigh had developed a mass of hair. How could that have happened? This was one effect of snakebite I had been unaware of. Yet closer inspection revealed the Detective had used his wig as a tourniquet. The wound was still gaping, however, and its lips were purple.

"Don't worry," he said, reading my thoughts. "It was only a harmless grass snake; it will heal in no time."

I became aware of Mormile hovering beside me.

"How about a little song, Freda, to raise the spirits a little. What do you say?"

I noticed he had a deep red rim running around his forehead.

I said, "No," and felt empowered, although my physical condition was still poor.

Throughout, the Detective's eyes were trained upon me. As if he was waiting for me to say or do something. I didn't want to disappoint him, but I didn't know what it was he was expecting.

The tempo of the music changed then, and Mormile himself took to the stage to sing, "Amore Arrivo." His voice wasn't bad considering he was an amateur.

"Dance?" Asked the Detective.

I nodded, although I could barely stand. Again he lifted me in those strong arms of his, and we took to the floor. One by one, the other couples melted away, leaving us alone in that trembling world, perfumed by his masculine aroma, warmed by the heat of his body so close to mine, and accompanied by the lilting notes of Mormile's song.

As the Detective's lips sought mine, I allowed my eyes to close, and I drifted into a state of what I can only describe as rapture.

eleven

When I next opened my eyes, I couldn't fathom where I was and what had happened to me. In the muted light, I couldn't see very much, but I knew I was in a bed. There were crisp sheets around me and the smell of antiseptic hung in the air. I could hear muffled crying and groans coming from close by. It dawned upon me that I was in hospital. In fact, as my eyes accustomed to the gloom, it began to feel very familiar. I couldn't be certain, but I thought it was the same ward I was in after the accident.

There were rows of beds opposite, and to my left and right, and in them were the forms of sleeping figures. Next to my bed was a locker with a fruit bowl and a vase of carnations on it. I noticed there was a drip pumping some colorless fluid into my arm.

Then I began to remember things. Of course, I had been bitten by a snake at the cabaret club, fallen off the stage, and inhaled smoke from the fire. I tried to move, but my bad leg, the same one that had been bitten, felt dead and heavy and wouldn't respond at all to my attempts to shift it. I pulled back the bedclothes and the hospital-issue surgical gown and was shocked to see that my leg and foot had gone green. Pea green. My thigh, where the bite was, was wrapped tightly in a bandage.

"Look at the color of that!" said a voice. It was the woman in the bed to the left, who lost no time in shuffling over to get a closer look. Both her arms were mummified in bandages and some of her hair had been singed off.

"Oooh," she continued, "isn't it horrible? Like something dredged up from a pond. Here, Nerissa, come and have a look at poor Signora Kapoor's leg."

Nerissa, who inhabited the bed opposite, struggled to rise. She was held rigid in a neck brace and in addition one of her feet was in plaster. Slowly, painfully, she crossed the ward, taking what seemed like ages to make the dozen or so steps.

She scrutinized my leg for some minutes in silence, before turning round and negotiating her way back again.

"Poor soul," said my neighbor as we watched Nerissa's retreat in slow motion, "bit off her own tongue in the crush.

Doctors tried to sew it back on, but it didn't take. Got it on upside down. First one they'd done, you see. Anyway she'll never speak again."

I was beginning to feel depressed.

"I'm Valeria, by the way," she continued. "You've been out cold for five days. I did enjoy your turn though, at the club. There's nothing left of it now, of course, razed to the ground. Shame really. Still that's the way things are, I suppose; here today, gone tomorrow."

I closed my eyes and feigned sleep. Hopefully, Valeria would go away and leave me alone. From time to time I felt the touch of her bandaged fingers against my bad leg, but I ignored them, and managed to drift off again.

While I was asleep, the doctor came in to make his round of the ward. He was an extraordinarily tall man, and had to stoop to avoid hitting his head on the lamps hanging from the ceiling. He wore the green cap of a surgeon, and much of his face was obscured by his face mask. He examined Nerissa, and was a little too quick in plunging his fingers into her mouth. Her overactive teeth couldn't help biting him.

Then the doctor crossed to the bed of my neighbor, Valeria. Although she was advanced in years, she did not hesitate in raising up her already skimpy negligee to reveal more of her crepey legs and assuming what she supposed to be a seductive pose on the counterpane. The doctor examined her singed eyebrows. Was he being overimaginative, or did her withered lips pucker up as though they were about to kiss him, despite the protecting presence of the mask? He couldn't take the risk, and, turning sharply, leaving Valeria gaping, came over to my bed.

One look from those dark eyes was enough to convince me that this wasn't the regular doctor. I knew it was the Detective, got up in another disguise.

"How are you feeling?" he asked, shining his penlight into each of my eyes in turn.

Yet the bright light was not that of the penlight of the doctor-detective; it was the reading light above my bed. I blinked my eyes, in the dull space between sleeping and waking, wondering how much of the dream was reality and how much had been conjured up by my own imagination.

Leaning over me was Dario Mormile, although it took me a little while to place him, as he had a sort of brass helmet on his head that came down low over his eyes, shading them, so that in order to look at anything he had to tilt his head backward and squint out from underneath it. He read my look of confusion.

"It's okay, Freda, it's me; it's a bass tuba," he explained. "That *puzzone* Selmo d'Angelo rammed it onto my head in the panic to escape the club. I spent seven hours in surgery, but they couldn't get it off. It's embedded itself into my skull. All they could do was saw off the rest, so at least now no one can play it. They say I'm going to have to live with it, but I want it gone. I'm going to go abroad, find a good doctor . . ."

I thought I was still dreaming, but as I looked around me I had the feeling I must be awake. Some of the patients, those who were well enough, sat around the central table eating a supper of what smelled like boiled veal and onions. There were visitors at some of the bedsides, and a number of nurses walking past with bedpans and bandages. Mormile chattered on, although I wasn't really listening to him.

"Freda, you know, I'm ruined now. Ruined. The club was destroyed by the fire. Totally. There's nothing left. Nothing. All those years of work, just gone up in smoke. The insurers say they'll pay me nothing. Some small print on the back of the policy. But I'll get even with them. Nobody messes with me. Some people are talking about lawsuits. Seven people died in there. And you know, Freda, I'm not blaming you, but it was all your fault."

"My fault?" I gasped. My voice sounded strange to me. Like someone else's. I had got out of the habit of speaking.

"Think about it," he said. "If it wasn't for you, none of this would have happened."

twelve

This time I woke up to find Signora Dorotea stroking my hand, with a worried look on her face.

"Is it really my fault?" I asked her.

"No, dear," she said. "Of course it's not your fault. It's that louse Mormile. I can't believe you took that job there. We said we'd help you with the money. Do you know, he had no insurance, and the fire escapes were blocked off? That's in addition to keeping dangerous reptiles on the premises. You are lucky to be alive. The police are out looking for him, and when they find him, believe me, they're going to throw the book at him. There are other people looking for him too. Angry people. Some very influential persons died that night, Freda—I know because we're doing the funerals—and lots more were injured. They want revenge. If the police find him first, he'll be lucky."

"But he's in here," I whispered. "In the hospital. I've seen him. He was here just now, before you arrived. He's got the bell of a bass tuba stuck on his head. The doctors can't get it off. He's going to have to live with it like that, but he says at least nobody can play it now. They've cut the mouthpiece off . . ."

"Of course, dear," said Signora Dorotea in the voice she used on deranged customers. "Now, the doctors have said you need a lot of rest. You've been very ill. The snake that bit you was a black mamba. By rights you shouldn't be here. But you're going to get better. So I just want you to lie quietly, and not get yourself excited. I've brought you some nice grapes, and look, here's a copy of *Mortician's Monthly* just out—I think you've come out lovely in the photo . . ."

"Nice grapes," I repeated for no reason, "lovely in the photo."

thirteen

"I remember you," said a voice at the foot of the bed.

I looked up. It was a nursing sister whom I vaguely remembered from before. Nurse Spada. She had big lips, like a fish, and a briny odor hung about her.

"Same leg, isn't it? Unlucky that. I was saying to your husband . . ."

"My husband?"

"Yes, the little fat fellow with the loud suits. Has a habit of throwing his voice. Seems devoted to you. He's been in every day, sitting by the bed, holding your hand."

"He's been here?" I asked, incredulous, horrified, confused.

"And the others," she added with a wink and a smirk, "but

don't worry, we've done our best to keep them from running into one another."

"Others?" I asked weakly. Was this hallucination the result of the snakebite, I wondered, or the medication they were giving me?

"You know . . ." Nurse Spada said, with another wink, and this time a nudge of her elbow, for she had approached the side of the bed.

"The big tall one, nice eyes. Some of the girls on the ward have got the hots for him, I can tell you. And then there's that other one, the strange fellow with the trumpet on his head."

"It's a tuba," I corrected her.

"Whatever." She shrugged. "Sidles about; here one minute, gone the next, shifty-like, always looking over his shoulder. There's even been a schoolboy here, once or twice, bit wooden, shiny, small, high-pitched voice. You certainly get the biggest share of gentlemen visitors. Some of the other ladies are quite jealous. Still, I suppose that comes of being in show business. I've read that celebrity is an 'aphrozodiac.' "

"Aphrodisiac," I corrected her again.

"My, we are precise, aren't we?" she said, and stalked off. Later I heard her telling the other nurses that I was so full of my own importance it was pointless talking to me. From then on they called me Miss High-and-Mighty. "Miss High-and-

Mighty needs a bedpan." "Time for Miss High-and-Mighty's medication."

She had to be wrong. How could Alberto have been here? What a horrible thought. I scrutinized my hand, looking for some trace of his greasy, fleshy touch upon it. There was none. I convinced myself the nurse was suffering delusions, and sank back into my pillows. Signora Dorotea was right; I needed rest.

fourteen

The following day, although I felt desperately tired, I willed myself to stay awake. If Alberto came again, I would catch him. When afternoon visiting began, I increased my vigilance. I was constantly on the watch, and scrutinized everybody who entered the ward to make sure no trick was being played on me.

Many men I recognized from the club came in from their ward down the corridor. Some of them had the most horrible injuries: missing eyes, arms, legs, teeth, ears; total body burns; and the various signs of crushing—indelible footprints on their heads, elongated bodies, mangled limbs.

I recognized Selmo d'Angelo, who had caused the tuba to become imbedded in Dario Mormile's head. Selmo and Labbra Fini, who played the trombone, were bandaged together tightly around the torso. It appeared their flesh had melted during the fire and the two of them had fused. It was unclear whether they could hope for a successful separation. They were visiting Labbra's lady friend, Lola, who was suffering from acute smoke inhalation, and the three of them were hotly debating their future sleeping arrangements for when they were discharged.

I spotted someone in a monkey costume, a magician, two nuns, an official photographer, and a vendor of rosaries, but I was ninety-nine percent certain Alberto had not managed to infiltrate the ward.

Finally a figure walked through the door that I knew. It was the Detective, and I wasn't imagining it this time. The nurses began acting like schoolgirls, giggling, and blushing and making lewd comments to one another. With two strides, he reached my bedside. He was holding a bunch of tired anemones. I put them in my beaker of water. Valeria, in the next bed, was already busily adjusting her wrinkled décolletage after applying an unnecessary amount of Springtime in Paris, which made everybody sneeze.

"How are you feeling?" he asked, predictably. The whole of the ward went suddenly silent.

"I feel that this isn't really me," I whispered, "that all of this is happening to somebody else."

"And how's the leg?"

"It's still green." I pulled up the covers to show him. I thought he had earned the right to see it. After all, he had saved my life. If he found the sight horrible, his face didn't show it. I was grateful for that. We lapsed into silence, as the rest of the ward started talking again.

"Just imagine the size of it!" I heard one of the nurses saying. Her colleagues laughed raucously and indecently.

"You can examine my legs any time you like!" called Valeria, exposing limbs that would not have looked out of place on a chicken.

The Detective sat down in the vinyl-covered chair next to my drip and locker. It emitted a loud squeak, and then a snort as the air was squeezed out of the cushion.

"You saved my life," I said, sounding like a character from a bad movie, but I couldn't help it; I had to say it. I meant it though; I wasn't acting. "If it wasn't for you, I would be dead."

He leaned in close. His scent filled my body. If I'd had the strength, I would have buried myself in him, regardless of the audience.

"Freda," he replied, so softly I hardly heard him, "I wasn't there that night, you understand? It's important."

Everybody else on the ward was straining to hear his words. And what they couldn't hear, they made up.

I nodded. I understood. But what I understood was nothing.

His face was so close it was almost touching mine. His lips were dry, soft, pink, parted. His breathing was slow. I don't know how long we stayed like that, but visiting time evaporated, and the spell was broken by chairs scraping on the floor, cries of "Get well soon," and Nurse Spada saying loudly, "Too bad the husband didn't come in today."

"They're saying Alberto has been in," I said, remembering, "but it can't be true, can it?"

The Detective opened his mesmerizing lips to speak. "We can't rule out any possibility." I felt the weight of each word, each minuscule puff of breath on my face, and preserved them as something precious.

Reluctantly, he stood up to leave. There was so much of him it was like the unfolding of a map. He gave me a look, which I preserved along with his breath, with his words, and tried to smile. Simultaneously we glanced at the anemones. They had wilted and their heads flopped over the edge of the glass, too heavy for their stems.

I watched the Detective's giant back retreating. It gave me pain to watch him leave me. At the exit, he turned, and searched for me among the rows of identical beds. All the ladies waved their hands, at least those who still had them did. Those that didn't raised what bandaged limbs they could muster in the circumstances. Even the nurses blew kisses.

Finally he ducked through the doorway and was gone.

fifteen

"Come on, Signora Kapoor," said Nurse Spada in my ear. "Time to wake up. The psychiatrist is here to see you, Dr. Piccante."

A round face, rosy and shiny as a little apple, was looking down at me. Perching on its upper lip was a mustache that looked like moss. Idly I wondered what had become of Dr. Boncoddo, but didn't want to ask. I didn't want to confess to a history of psychiatric involvement.

Dr. Piccante glanced down at a folder with my stage name on it. Then he looked at me and smiled.

"So how long have you been having these hallucinations, Signora Kapoor?"

My look must have been as blank as the sheets, because he continued talking:

"These erotic fantasies about a detective, Signor"—ruffling among his papers for the name—"ah, yes, Balbini?

"The delusions about a small, fat man with a hairpiece and a ventriloquist's dummy? Parrots crop up a lot too. About performing as a cabaret singer in a nightclub of dubious repute? What is it, the Pussy Cat Lounge? Oh, no, the Berenice, yes. Dreadful place—we had the departmental Christmas party there once. Never again. The nightclub proprietor, one Dario Mormile. Snakes. Venom. Fires. The old familiar stuff. The list goes on and on," he concluded, shuffling through the sheaf.

"But they're not delusions," I said. "This is my life."

"Ahh, Signora Kapoor, if you only knew how many of my patients have used that immortal line. Now, tell me, apart from the fantasy cabaret act, what do you really do for a living?"

"I'm an embalmer."

He nodded enthusiastically. "Now, would you say you've been overdoing it a bit recently? Bodies been piling up, have they?"

Now it was my turn to nod. I thought he was waiting for it, and it would seem churlish not to.

"Thought so. Yes, you've been feeling a little strained. Finding it hard to cope. I can tell. And it's nothing to be ashamed of. Absolutely not. Get that idea out of your head.

Shoo! There, now it's gone! Now, what you need, Signora Kapoor, Veronique—if you will allow me—is a holiday. Get some rest. Enjoy the sun. Take that bikini out of mothballs. Ever thought of a Mediterranean cruise? They can be very beneficial in these circumstances. Sea breezes. Jolly sailors. You know the sort of thing . . ."

From Now On

one

I felt like Sleeping Beauty coming alive again after a sleep of one hundred years. When I came round from the coma, I was seized with an overwhelming feeling of urgency. I had wasted so much time. I had so much life to live, and I had to get on with it. I needed to get back to work. I needed sex, and I was going to get it.

In my locker I found a blue sequined dress and silver shoes—I didn't know who they belonged to, but I put them on anyway. I ripped back the curtains around my bed, and came face-to-face with Fiamma, giving her a start. She had just returned from a tour of African nations, and was covered in mosquito bites. The Secret Service had sealed off the ward, which caused a bit of a stir, and lots of square-shaped men were standing around in dark suits and sunglasses.

"I'm getting out of here," I said.

"They told me you were near death."

"No," I corrected her, "I was only near life."

Immediately Fiamma sent one of her people in search of a pair of crutches, which, when they arrived, gave me a curious sense of déjà vu. She had someone else pack up the contents of my locker. There wasn't much: a used frosted-pink lipstick called First Kiss, a comb with many of the teeth missing and some blond hairs running through it, a pair of graying underpants, a bottle of hair restorer, and a bruised and puckered apple. These things didn't even belong to me, so I put them in the trash.

Nurse Spada, who had fought her way through the security cordon and wasn't happy, rushed over. "You can't go. The doctors haven't discharged you."

"I'm going," I said simply, and hauled myself away to freedom.

In the long corridor that led to the exit, I passed a pajama-wearing figure I hadn't seen in a long time.

"Signor Tontini," I said. "How are you?"

As I watched, my downstairs neighbor went a vivid shade of red. He clutched his chest and fell to the floor. Doctors and nurses rushed in from all directions. He was gathered up and placed on a gurney. His dentures were removed, and continued to chatter on the palm of the junior nurse entrusted with their care. Two of the doctors started to perform cardiac massage as he was rushed off to the emergency room, while his family was being traced and a priest summoned.

Poor Signor Tontini. His rage had been killing him for years. Now it seemed to have finally succeeded.

It was strange to be out in the world again. The sun was blinding and so hot I could feel it braising my bare shoulders like a blowtorch. The sky was bluer than it had ever been. As we drove along, the streets appeared more crowded, the traffic more chaotic, and the buildings more imposing than I remembered. I watched out of the window of the limousine, feeling like a tourist, and full of joy that I was alive.

Fiamma dropped me at my apartment and then drove on to the Ministry to take part in the daily conference call from the prime minister. There were several letters waiting for me on my doormat, which was unusual because I hardly ever got any mail. I didn't notice at the time that a picture postcard had got pushed under the mat, and I didn't find it until long afterward.

One letter was franked "Destino Assicurazione." Idly I tore it open. It was probably only an advertisement urging me to take out a policy. But it wasn't. I looked at the date—August 18, 1975—I had lost almost a month, possibly more—the letter could have been lying there for some time. I read on:

> Dear Madam,
>
> Re: LIPPI, one Alberto Geronimo
>
> Following satisfactory conclusions of our investigations, we enclose a check for the amount thirty million lire, in respect of life insurance policy on the above named, ref LIPAG177.
>
> Assuring you of our best attentions at all times,
> Signed: [undecipherable squiggle]
> For Destino Assicurazione

So Alberto was dead! Really dead. He had to be. I knew insurance companies would never pay out if there was the slightest glimmer of doubt. They had conducted thorough investigations. They had proof Alberto was dead. At last I finally knew the truth. Immediately I called Signora Dorotea—I had to tell somebody. She was amazed I was out of hospital.

"I was there just last night," she said. "You were sleeping like a stone."

"Well, I'm awake now," I said, "and guess what?" I read her the letter.

"Of course he's dead," she said. "I always knew he was—felt it in my bones. We'll go and light a candle for him—poor soul—although I never liked the man, I wished him no harm, and it's a dreadful thing to have happened."

I hung up and opened another of the letters. It was from the bank, apologizing for their error, informing me that my account was now unfrozen, offering me their condolences on Alberto's death and promising me a mystery free gift in compensation. That they could keep—I had had enough mysteries recently to last my whole lifetime.

The final envelope bore the crest of the Ventriloquists' Benevolent Association. Along with a letter of sympathy for my great loss, there was a check for a million lire, and a page torn out of *Ventriloquism Today* headed "Obituaries." It read: "LIPPI Alberto Geronimo April 1, 1942–July 19, 1975. All in the profession will mourn the passing in tragic circumstances of our brother ventriloquist Alberto Lippi. Short and fat with an outstanding talent, he was a regular performer at that world-famous haunt of celebrities, the exclusive Berenice cabaret club. A favorite on the cruise-liner circuit, Lippi was also a popular choice for kiddies' parties. He is survived by the mischievous schoolboy Malco. Any member of the Guild able to provide a suitable opening for the dummy should contact the Secretary."

Now that I knew Alberto wasn't coming back, I could almost begin to feel sorry for him, but when I heard a key turning in the lock to my front door, any charitable thoughts evaporated and I was ready to have a heart attack.

two

A head poked its way around the door. A man's head. It wasn't Alberto, and I was able to start breathing again. He's dead, I told myself; he'll never come back. I had to rid myself of the irrational fear that he was going to reappear.

The man wasn't completely unknown to me. I had definitely seen him before somewhere. Now, where was it? Work? The hospital? The Berenice? The market? More important, what was he doing in my apartment?

"Ciao, bella!" He said, and his body followed his head into the passage. "I'm Nello."

Uninvited, he came to join me in the parlor.

"Nello?"

"Nello Tontini. From downstairs. Nabore's boy. Saw through the hole that you were back."

So that's where I had seen him before. The son of Signor Tontini. He had an air of confidence about him—even the hairs at his neck and on his arms sprouted a cocky growth. The look of a man to whom life came easily.

"Freda, isn't it?"

I nodded.

"Pretty dress."

"Thanks."

"Thing is, I've been looking through a few of Papa's things," he went on; "seems there are some irregularities . . ."

His words trailed off, and he came up very close. His aftershave was eye-stinging.

"Do you know, Freda," he said, touching me lightly on the arm, "that the rent on this apartment hasn't been paid for eight weeks?"

"The rent!" I exclaimed. "Of course! I forgot all about it. I'll write you out a check at once."

"No rush," he replied. "I'm sure we can come to some arrangement. You're an attractive woman, Freda." With his fingertip he began tracing a line from my shoulder down my arm.

"Too bad they're looking for you at the hospital," I said. "I just came from there. Your pa has taken a turn for the worst."

Reluctantly he gave me back my arm and turned to go.

As he let himself out, he said, huskily, "I meant what I said, Freda; think it over. But don't let the grass grow under your feet."

I wanted to laugh. Nello was repulsive, but still I puckered at the recollection of his touch. In the mirror I looked at my reflection, and almost didn't recognize myself. I looked better than I ever had. It must have been sleeping all that time. He was right, I was an attractive woman—and the thought was entirely new to me. I'd always considered myself plain. The sparkly dress really suited me, and I wriggled around in front of the mirror, admiring my new sexy look.

I threw open the windows to let in some fresh air and eradicate the pervading stench of Nello Tontini's Conqueror aftershave. Then I pulled all my boring middle-aged clothes out of the closet. They would have to go: from now on I was going to be a different person. One by one I flung them out of the window and waved as they sailed away on the breeze. Dull old Freda Lippi flapped away along with them. Exciting, daring, Freda Castro was being reborn.

In the Campo the market was whirling with life, and the raucous cries of the merchants competed with one another.

"Water pistols."

"Ever-youthful face cream."

"Rabbits, tender and cheap."

As I stood idly watching a barrow brimming with brilliant lemons bumping along the street, there was a flurry of air and bright blue feathers and Pierino landed on the window ledge.

"Mamma," he cried. "Mamma."

My shriek of joy made everybody beneath look up.

"Pierino!"

I held out my hand and he hopped onto it. At last he had come home. To my amazement there was more fluttering, and another parrot, blue but with a little yellow tuft on top of its head, landed on the sill.

"Sweetheart," Pierino explained.

"Ahhh," I said. "Sweetheart."

The new parrot also hopped onto my hand. "Gloria," she said shyly. "Glorrrrrrria."

Then the two of them flew into the cage, where they sat side by side on the perch billing and cooing.

I was so excited I had to call Signora Dorotea again.

"I told you he'd come back," she said, predictably. "Wasn't I right?"

I also called Fiamma, but she was still on the conference call, so I left a message with the secretary, who promised to pass her a note. Lastly, I called Uncle Birillo. Aunt Ninfa answered and she sounded upset. In fact, she was honking into the phone great racking sobs.

"Freda, he's left me," she bellowed, "for that *puttana* Mimosa Pernice. You see, I was right. I was right all along . . ." Here there was a sound like an elephant trumpeting, and her hairdresser, Raffaello, took over the phone to say Aunt Ninfa had collapsed.

So I was wrong: Uncle Birillo *was* the type of man to have a mistress. I felt sorry for Aunt Ninfa, but my uncle was right—experience had taught me there's no sense in staying in a marriage with someone you don't like.

Pierino pulled the cover down over the cage, and taking the hint, I decided to go out, but made sure I shut all the windows first.

My leg was already feeling much better, and halfway along the block I handed my crutches to a lame beggar with too many fingers on his right hand. By coincidence it was the same beggar I had given my first pair of crutches to, nine years before, and they had only just worn out. I wished him well but hoped these were the last pair he would be getting from me.

My first stop was the Parrucchiere Mimmo, and three hours later I emerged with an enormous Afro perm that was then all the rage. I was met by a chorus of wolf whistles from passing pastry cooks and butchers' boys, and several of the slow-moving trucks on the street sounded their horns.

From there I sashayed into Moda Seduttrice and spent the next couple of hours trying on everything in the shop. I left with seven shopping bags stuffed with sparkly evening wear and a selection of exotic lingerie in bold colors. I also bought two halter-neck sundresses, three tight blouses with giant collars, some hip-hugger pants, a plaid poncho, and a macramé belt, which I thought offered an alluring but practical range of options for day wear.

My final purchases were a bottle of wine, a big bar of chocolate, a jar of Pure Passion bath oil, and a book entitled *Aphrodisiac Foods: Fifty Recipes for a Raunchy Evening*.

I walked home through the market, which was now closing up, and saw that Perdita Stellata was selling my old clothes on her stall. The funeral suit in which I had married Alberto was being offered for five hundred lire. On a rail marked "Bargains" was the purple nylon dress I had worn to meet his mother. That life seemed so long ago now. I regarded the Freda I was then with a mixture of disbelief, exasperation, and indulgence, like an embarrassing younger sister. I felt older, but at the same time, more youthful, released from the double burden of premature middle age and stolid immaturity.

Inside, the lovebirds were busy feathering their nest with plundered fluff, cotton flocks, torn paper, and shredded scraps from the curtains. Soon Gloria was to lay four white eggs, and the two of them were as proud and pleased as any human parents.

I put on some music, poured myself a glass of wine, opened the chocolate, and sprawled on the bed. Through the slit in my skirt I noticed my leg was no longer green—it had faded to a pleasant yellow color, and I hoped by the next day it would look almost normal. I sipped the wine and flipped through the cookbook. Then I called the Detective.

"Balbini," he said, and immediately I felt deliciously warm and moist.

"Dinner," I breathed into the phone, "tomorrow at eight." Then I hung up. There was no need to say more.

Early the next morning I went down to the market and filled two baskets with provisions. I bought the hottest chilies I could find, ripe tomatoes, garlic, onions, a big bunch of basil, and some salad leaves. From the fishmonger, Selmo Manfredi (who didn't recognize me and called me Barbara, although I had known him for years), I got some wonderful eels, which swam around happily in their plastic bag of water. I bought fresh *maccheroni* at the Pastificio Gobbo, and eggs from the chicken man. Lastly, I picked up two bottles of red wine, a box of candles, a bunch of marigolds for the table, and fruit: nectarines, figs, apricots, strawberries, and cherries.

When I arrived at work, Signora Dorotea didn't recognize me either initially, and thought I was a customer wanting to arrange a funeral.

"Freda, what's happened to your hair?" she screamed. "Looks like you've had an electric shock."

"It's the latest thing," I said, but I don't think she was convinced.

It was so good to be back. We sat over a cup of coffee and some pastries, and caught up on everything that had happened. I told her the staggering news that Uncle Birillo had left Aunt Ninfa for someone called Mimosa Pernice.

"Sometimes, Freda, I think you go around with your eyes shut," she said. "He's been seeing her since 1957 to my certain knowledge."

"Sometimes," I replied, "you think you know everything. But there's one thing you definitely don't know."

"What's that?" she asked, her eyes gleaming with impatience to hear the gossip.

"You don't know who's coming to have dinner with me tonight."

"Ooooooh," she said, delighted. "I think I can guess!"

Just then the telephone on the desk rang, and Signora Dorotea picked it up.

"Onranze Funebri Pompi," she announced in her deep

business voice. After a pause she added, "Just one moment," and handed me the receiver.

"Freda?" came a voice I immediately recognized.

"I came through for you, didn't I? All it took was a few phone calls from me. Now, one good turn deserves another. I'll rub yours if you rub mine and all that. I got a stiff sitting here, see, and it needs to disappear, no questions asked, and I think to myself, Freda's the girl to help me out here . . ."

"No," I said loudly. "No, no, no." And then I put the phone down.

Signora Dorotea sent me off early to prepare myself, and by six I was in my little kitchen brewing the hottest chili sauce in history. *Aphrodisiac Foods* assured me the hotter the chili, the more fiery the passion—so I was taking no chances and chopped five big ones and sautéed them in oil with an onion and a lot of garlic. Then I added my sun-ripened tomatoes, salt, and torn leaves of basil. I left it cooking slowly on a low heat, and soon the intoxicating perfume was drifting through the apartment and out into the street causing passersby to raise their noses into the air.

The *maccheroni*, in its white paper bag, was set by the stove and would be plunged into boiling water at the last minute. This would be combined with the sauce and served for the first course.

Next, the eels, which I had been keeping in the bathroom basin. Grasping each in turn, I killed them by delivering them a smart blow to the back of the head with the rolling pin. Then I skinned them, gutted them, gave them a brisk rub down with a cloth to remove their shine, and sliced them into chunks. Interspersed with coarse sea salt and fresh bay leaves, they would roast gently in the oven, releasing their sumptuous perfume. "Eels, as everybody knows, are a potent aphrodisiac," announced the recipe book. "Serve these to your lover and wait for the temperature to rise."

Finally I washed and dried my wild salad leaves and arranged them on a platter and piled the succulent fruits into a dish.

Then I set the table and put the marigolds in the center, dotted a few candles around the room, put a record on the stereo, and opened the wine to breathe. I stood back to admire my handiwork, and I do think I had arranged it all rather well.

I had an hour left to prepare myself. First, I took a hot deep bath to which I added a long draft of Pure Passion (*guaranteed to promote lust,* it said on the label, *or your money back*). I raised my leg and looked at it closely. It was as strong now as it ever was. The color had returned to normal, and the wound where the snake bit me was now scarcely visible. I knew that at last I would be having sex, and I could hardly control myself at the thought of it. Although I had been waiting twenty-six years and approximately seventy-eight days, I honestly didn't think I could wait a moment longer.

I got out before I began to pucker, dried, rubbed in lotion, stirred the tomato sauce, and generally wandered about naked singing to myself with a delicious feeling of anticipation bubbling up inside me. It was now seven-forty and I knew I had to get dressed. In the bedroom I looked straight into another eye through the hole in the floor. Nello Tontini. Peeping Tom. Well, let him look. I didn't care. In fact I jiggled about a bit provocatively on purpose.

I had it in mind to wear the long red dress with the plunging neckline and the thigh-high slit in the skirt, together with the very flimsy coordinating underwear. Nello Tontini approved. I could tell by the steam rising up through the hole. I just had time to fling on a pair of shoes, slick on some lipstick, fluff out the perm, and light the candles before there was a tap on the door.

Sure enough, it was the Detective. He lurched when he saw me.

"Freda," he gasped, "you look different."

"It's my hair," I replied. "I had it done."

He came inside, and his intoxicating aroma overwhelmed

me. The smoldering look in his dark eyes showed me I wouldn't be disappointed. He was wearing a smart black suit, and a pink shirt with an open collar. He handed me a box of chocolates.

In the parlor, Pierino and Gloria were intent on their courtship rituals on the back of the sofa. She had ruffled her feathers, and he was preening them gently. I turned on the music—a Brazilian samba—which they seemed to like. Perhaps it reminded them of home.

"Dance?" I asked the Detective.

And we began to move, sometimes holding each other close—and his body felt hard and strong and warm—and sometimes, when the music dictated, at arm's length, twirling and shimmying in time to the beat. The Detective was an excellent dancer, I have to say—he was very fast on his feet for a man his height, and he had a natural rhythm. When we finally came to a halt, breathless and laughing, I noticed the parrots had broken off their nibbling, and were looking at us in astonishment.

Now that the initial ice had melted, we chatted with ease about work, the weather, the trials of city life in the summer heat. I poured him a glass of wine. The food was almost ready.

By candlelight I served the first course of *maccheroni all'arrabbiata,* and watched intently as the Detective raised the initial forkful to his lips. Soon tears came into his eyes and his nose began to stream.

"It's," he gasped, "very"—then he started coughing, and hurried to swallow his wine—"good," he spluttered. "Hot"—pant—"just how I"—croak—"like it."

"I like it hot too," I said, looking deep into his eyes, and at the same time licking my lips ostentatiously. Now it was my turn to taste the dish. I put a morsel into my mouth and immediately felt the most intense burning sensation as it exploded on my tongue, set fire to my gums, and scalded my throat.

I ran into the kitchen, spat into the garbage, and stuck my head, with my mouth open, under the tap.

The Detective followed me in. "Are you all right?" he asked. "Can I get you a glass?" He went to the cupboard and reached one down (it seemed he knew where everything was, but of course he had already conducted a thorough search of the place). While I tried to cool my ravaged throat—I now knew just how a trainee fire-eater feels—the Detective flipped through *Aphrodisiac Foods* with a smile on his chili-stung lips.

"I think," I said in a strange strangulated voice, "we'll move right along to the main course."

I opened the oven and reached in for the eels. Their

bulging eyes looked at me with reproach. I could feel the Detective standing close behind me, and the air between our two bodies was fizzing with electricity.

I had the Detective carry in the salad while I followed with the eels.

"Mmmmm, Freda, these are amazing," he said with his mouth full. "You know, I read somewhere once that eels are a powerful aphrodisiac."

"Is that right?" I replied. "I didn't know that."

Whether it was true or not, they were certainly delicious, and we soon ate them all up.

The light outside began to fade. The room grew warmer. The Detective removed his jacket, releasing more of his seductive body odor. The wine somehow disappeared from both bottles.

We moved on to the fruit, and the Detective fed me a segment of nectarine across the table with his fingers. I opened my mouth and allowed him to put it inside. It was a perfect fruit, so juicy, and soft, and felt so good on my swollen tongue. Some of the juice escaped from my lips and trickled down into my cleavage.

"Allow me," murmured the Detective.

He came and knelt at my side, and started licking the glistening trail of juice. When his tongue touched my skin, involuntarily I shot up into the air. It was the most erotic experience of my entire life. I sprawled back in my chair with abandon and allowed the Detective to lick every bit of exposed flesh (I have to confess I even tried to expose more of it by pulling surreptitiously at my dress). Often I let out little gasps and squeals of delight—I couldn't help myself.

I felt like a double bass feels when its very deepest notes are being played. There was the plucking of a string—a resonating—in my groin that was making me lurch. I grabbed hold of the Detective's head and pulled his mouth toward mine. We began kissing with such passion that my chair tipped over backward and we fell to the floor with a crash. Thankfully neither of us was hurt, and we were able to laugh about it.

Quickly, anxious not to lose the moment, I climbed on top of him, held his face between my hands, and pressed my lips hard into his. Oh, his kisses were electrifying! I had to have so many of them. All of them. I never wanted them to stop. It was all so urgent. I was seized with a kind of desperation I could never have imagined before this moment.

I knew I had to get his clothes off. And I had to get them off right now. It couldn't wait. I ripped off his shirt, then fought with his pants, thrashing and flailing with a determination he found funny.

I tore off my own dress, sending a cloud of sequins tinkling into the air, and unencumbered by the long skirt, I was able to get more of a grip on the Detective's underwear.

At last he was naked, and I feasted my eyes upon him. His willy was the most magnificent thing I had ever seen. It was twice the size of Ernesto Porcino's, and I couldn't wait to sample its delights.

I reached toward it. At this precise moment a key turned in the front door. If it was Nello Tontini, I would murder him with an ax. Then Pierino started squawking madly and flapping his wings,

"Papa!" he shrieked. "Papa's home!"

Acknowledgments

A big thank you to:

The inspirational Roger Gillman, and the staff at Gillman's Funeral Service

The unparalleled Julia Serebrinsky

The dauntless duo, Jean Naggar and Jennifer Weltz

The incredible Christopher Prior